WELCOME TO ANDIE'S WORLD . . .

Andie sat across the desk from Mr. Donnelly, the dean. He said, "Andie, you've got a couple of months left. You're doing extremely well in your courses. Your chances for a scholarship are excellent—"

"I know, Mr. Donnelly."

"Then what is your problem?"

"I guess I got fed up. Or worn down. Or something."

"With what?"

"With the way we get treated."

"Who's we?"

Andie shook her head. "Oh, come on," she said, "you know who."

The dean cleared his throat. "As long as the structure of this community remains as it is, there are going to be haves and have-nots getting their education side by side."

Andie glared at him. "Don't call me a have-not, Mr. Donnelly," she said coldly. "You can call me a freak or a zoid, but not a have-not!"

PARAMOUNT PICTURES PRESENTS
A JOHN HUGHES PRODUCTION
PRETTY IN PINK
MOLLY RINGWALD
HARRY DEAN STANTON
JON CRYER
ANNIE POTTS
JAMES SPADER
and ANDREW M^cCARTHY
Executive Producers
JOHN HUGHES and MICHAEL CHINICH
Written by JOHN HUGHES
Produced by LAUREN SHULER
Directed by HOWARD DEUTCH
A PARAMOUNT PICTURE

Pretty in Pink

A Novel by H. B. Gilmour
Based on the screenplay
by John Hughes

BANTAM BOOKS
TORONTO • NEW YORK • LONDON • SYDNEY • AUCKLAND

RL 6, IL age 11 and up

PRETTY IN PINK
A Bantam Book / March 1986

ISBN 0-553-25944-X

Published simultaneously in the United States and Canada

PRINTED IN THE UNITED STATES OF AMERICA
O   0 9 8 7 6 5 4 3 2 1

For Jessi, Jerry, and Judy.
For Noël, Suzanne, and Sukari.
And for the Evols of Bayside, Queens.
Especially Rocky. With love.

One

Andie Walsh didn't want to get out of bed. She thought she'd snuggle there awhile and wait for her mother to bring in her breakfast and open the shutters. Then daylight would warm her. The sweet spring air would stir the curtains in Andie's pink-and-white bedroom and rub like a silky cat against her mother's pink gown.

Andie Walsh's mother loved the color pink. Even her gardening gloves were pink, the ones she wore each morning when she chose the perfect pink rose for her daughter's breakfast tray.

Andie's mother was even more beautiful than a rose. She had creamy skin, thick chestnut-brown hair, and big brown eyes with velvety brown lashes that could brush away tears and time.

And she was cheerful in the morning. She was as cheerful in the morning as she was caring and gentle in the middle of the night, which was when she sat beside her daughter's bed talking quietly. She'd talk about where she'd been and why she'd stayed away so long

1

and how much she had missed Andie and how happy she was, at last, to be home.

Andie stirred under the cool caress of her mother's hand and sighed. "What I don't understand," she whispered, "is why—?"

And then the alarm clock went off, the way it always did. Andie's big brown eyes flew open, and the sigh caught in her throat as she realized her unfinished question would never be answered.

She hit the alarm clock with the flat of her hand.

Daylight was fighting its way through the factory grime that clung to the windows of the one-story bungalow where she and her father lived.

The filtered gray light crept like a burglar through her room. It touched the chipped pink furniture, the portrait of her mother in its oval frame beside her bed, the Picasso reproduction taped to a cracked wall, the curled edges of photographs tucked into a mirror frame. It glided over the textbooks on the desk and, on the dresser, the pots of gloss and blush, pencils and brushes, shades and shadows of makeup— blue, brown, green, and burgundy but, mostly, pink.

The gray light ransacked the odd assortment of old clothes and glittering costume jewelry, the corner heap of strange shoes and boots, the pink slips and camisoles and stock-

2

ings hung over the back of a chair. It swept across the big newsprint sketchpad filled with fashion drawings in which the thriftshop fabrics and accessories scattered around Andie's room had been transformed into fabulous creations, fantasies of *haute couture* street chic.

With a groan Andie dragged herself out of bed. Squinting and stumbling through the gray dawn light, she began to assemble her costume for the school day. Ace, her old dog, watched from under the bed.

From the jumble on her dresser Andie plucked a pair of hoop earrings and a bright pin—a junkshop treasure just the right size to cover the hole in the sleeve of her favorite jacket. Pink stockings draped over her arm, antique skirt over her shoulder, she caught her reflection in the dresser mirror.

It surprised her. Her eyes were still puffy and her hair was rumpled, but the girl in the mirror didn't look half bad. Andie thought of Duckie Dale suddenly, and smiled.

Yesterday, at school, he'd crept up behind her as she was studying her face in the mirror on the back of her locker door. She should have known he'd say something weird. Old Ducks— her demented, devoted, dependably freaky childhood pal. She'd known him for eight years now, since fourth grade. And she loved him . . . probably just a shade more than she dreaded running into him in the crowded school corridors where his madness seemed to flourish most.

"Oh, man, Andie," he'd said, peering over her shoulder. "Listen, can I borrow your mirror? There's something wrong with mine. Every time I look in it, I see this ultrastrange dude in reflector glasses and mile-high hair. Your mirror's got everything I ever wanted—a tall, willowy, almond-eyed, auburn-haired beauty. Aw, come on, Andie, just let me borrow it!"

Then, to her horror, Duckie had fallen to his knees. "Please, Andie," he'd begged, oblivious to the contemptuous snickers and icy stares of the school's so-called normal population—kids with credit cards, sports cars, and trendy clothes. Andie had rolled her eyes and blushed for both of them.

But here it was a day later, and there was Duckie's vision of her staring back from the dresser mirror. Tall and willowy, almond-eyed . . . and not half bad.

It wasn't every morning Andie Walsh could study herself with such satisfaction. Usually she looked in the mirror and shook her head in despair. Lips too big, nose too little, eyes blah-brown and crinkly at the corners. No cheekbones to speak of. No magic. No mystery.

Sometimes she'd look at herself, and then she'd look at the old photograph of the girl in the pink gown, and she'd say to the girl: "What do you think? Is this a face only a mother could love, or what?"

Automatically Andie's eyes sought the photograph now. It was one of the old photographs

4

tucked into the mirror frame, a faded souvenir of the 1960s—a snapshot of a girl with thick chestnut-brown hair and big brown eyes, a girl in a tacky pink prom gown.

The picture was torn. Long ago it had been torn in half so that only the pretty girl remained. All that was visible of her date was the pale, awkward hand at her waist.

Andie reached for the photograph, then changed her mind. At the last moment, her fingers moved from the girl's smiling face to the boy's pale hand. Sometimes Andie dreamed that it was her father's hand holding the waist of the girl in the pink prom gown. It wasn't, of course. It couldn't be. Her father hadn't met the girl—Andie's mother—until years later. And the missing half of the picture had probably been lost or destroyed by then.

Andie figured it was the girl in the prom gown who'd ripped the photograph in half. Of course she didn't know for sure. She hadn't found the photograph until after her mother had walked out, so she'd never had a chance to ask. But Andie knew the girl was good at getting rid of things she didn't need or want—trimming from her life, as she had from the photograph, what no longer mattered to her.

"What do you think? Not bad, right?" Andie asked the girl in the pink gown. "Maybe not a genuine almond-eyed, auburn-haired beauty yet, but worth the wait. See what you missed? Shame you couldn't stick around."

The factory whistle sounded at the plant on the other side of the railroad trestle. Andie heard the cars and trucks rumbling by, pebbles skidding beneath their wheels and clattering against the rickety, peeling wood of the front fence. And she knew the girl in the picture wouldn't think she'd missed all that much.

"Daddy, it's time to get up," Andie called on her way to the bathroom. It was almost seven-thirty when she emerged, showered and dressed. Down the hall, the door to her father's room was still shut. She fixed a pot of coffee and poured a cup for him.

"Daddy," she called again, opening his door. The stale smell of beer and cigarettes hit her along with the sight of her sleeping father lying unshaven on his rumpled bed in an undershirt and boxer shorts.

She flashed the light switch and he stirred slightly.

"Dad! Come on," she said. "It's seven-thirty!"

Slowly Jack Walsh began to wake up. He coughed. It was a deep, ugly cough. As he turned, trying to pull up the twisted sheets, Andie frowned with concern.

"I made you coffee," she said.

Jack nodded, his eyes still closed. "Thanks."

"I want you to go drink it. Then I want you to take a shower. Then I want you to get dressed.

Then I want you to go see that guy about the job. Okay?"

Jack smiled and nodded. Then he coughed again. "What would I do without you nagging me all the time?" he asked when he'd caught his breath.

He opened his eyes. Andie stood up quickly, a guilty look on her face. She stepped back from the side of his bed, where she'd just dipped the two cigarettes left in his crumpled pack into the glass of beer he'd left sitting on the floor last night. "You really want me to answer that?" she asked.

"No. Everything okay with you?" Jack squinted at her. "My God," he said suddenly, his voice husky—hung over, she thought. "Look at you. You're like Christmas walking into a room. How tall are you now?"

Andie shrugged.

"I've been getting in kind of late. We haven't talked much," Jack said. "What do you call those earrings?"

"Hoops," she said, touching the big old gypsy hoops she'd dug out of the basket on her dresser. "Anyway, there hasn't been much to say."

"School good?"

"No," Andie said, "but it never is."

"You're not having trouble with your grades, are you?" her father asked, genuinely surprised.

She shook her head. "It's not the work.

It's—" He started to cough again and she murmured, "Nothing. It's nothing."

Andie knew that she wouldn't check the mirror again before she left for school. She knew that just the thought of school had transformed her from a willowy almond-eyed beauty to a ragpile with a great sense of style. It must have been the dream she'd had this morning that had made her feel special and look special to herself—the dream of living in a beautiful house with smooth walls and splendid furniture, and having a garden in which pink roses grew, and having a mother; and having, just having.

"Did you get asked to the Prom yet?" her father asked.

Andie flinched. He'd inadvertently hit on a tender subject. Then she smiled quickly for him and shook her head.

"You will," Jack said earnestly. "When was the last time I told you how pretty you are?"

"About two minutes ago. Don't embarrass me." Andie laughed and hurried to the door. Then she stopped and turned to him. "Get up, okay? I really want you to do this today."

Jack looked at her and dropped his eyes. "I'm perfectly happy doing what I'm doing, you know."

"You're happy with part-time work?"

"You're right," Jack said. "That's why I'm getting up." He laughed, then coughed again.

Andie frowned at the cough. "I've got to go.

I'll be late," she said. She threw him a kiss, gave Ace a goodbye pat, and left.

Jack picked up his cigarettes as she ran down the hall. He tried to pull one from the soaking pack. "Oh, crap! Andie!" he hollered.

He heard the screen door slam. And then the grinding, whining, coughing noise of her ancient purple Kharman Ghia starting up in the driveway—a noise not unlike his own morning hack. As the car caught and began to back out of the driveway, he heard his daughter shout, "I love you! Get up!"

TWO

*B*lane McDonough leaned against the wall and pretended to be studying his schedule card. He'd look up now and then, to give a thumbs-up sign to someone who called out, "Hey, how's it goin', Blane-babe?" or to offer a smile to one of the future country club wives. These were the kids he'd grown up with: the richies, the kids who lived in the beautiful houses on the Lake. Not that Blane would have called them richies, of course. He didn't need to. He was one of them. He'd drunk his first hard liquor at their fathers' well-stocked bars, grabbed a Coke and micro-waved a burger in the designer kitchens their mothers occasionally visited.

But the real object of his attention now was someone outside the charmed circle of his youth. There were the richies, and then there were the zoids: the freaks, the outsiders, the zombies. And the girl he was looking at now was definitely a zoid.

Blane checked out the corridor to be sure none of the kids he knew was watching him watch her. She was fantastic-looking. She had short hair that was a kind of reddish cinnamon-brown color, and today she was wearing hoop earrings big enough to swing a pair of parrots on. He loved watching her. Loved the way she moved, the way she walked. Whether she was wearing her delicate, old-fashioned lace-up boots or heavy-soled workboots, she had an amazing little skip to her walk—an optimistic bounce, a kind of pride as unique and personal as the way she put herself together each day. It purely knocked him out. Leather and lace. Velvet and velcro.

He'd been watching her for some time. About two years, actually. He'd had his eye on her for close to that now, Blane figured. And here he was gearing up for graduation and she'd never even looked at him or noticed him checking her out. Not that he'd wanted her to. Not that he wanted her to see him looking at her now. Not that he wanted *anyone* to notice him noticing her—particularly not Cinderella's stepsisters, Kate and Benny, who were coming down the hall at that very moment.

Books piled up in one arm, chin resting on top of the pile and one knee raised for balance, Andie tried the combination to her locker for the third time.

"Got a match, zoid?" a brunette in three hundred dollars' worth of Ralph Lauren asked in passing.

"A match?" said the brunette's Calvin-clad

friend, looking Andie over with an amused smile. "Get serious, Kate. The zoid's wearing J.C. Penney's entire spring catalog. She's got no match."

Andie closed her eyes and gritted her teeth.

"Yeah, J.C. Penney's Salvation Army outlet. Steff ask you to the Prom yet, Benny?" Andie heard the Calvin girl ask.

"No," Benny-the-brunette replied, "but he will—"

"Excuse me, ladies."

Andie opened one eye cautiously at the sound of the familiar voice.

There was Duckie Dale lifting his skinny-brimmed hat to the horrified richies, his dark eyes hidden behind huge reflective shades, his grin big and broad.

"Oh, God!" Benny groaned. "It's the King of the Weirdos."

"What's he want?" whined Kate. They both shrank back as Duckie flung open his oversized coat and flapped the edges at them. Under it he was wearing a t-shirt, Bermuda shorts, plaid suspenders, unlaced hightop sneakers, and droopy black socks.

"We're having a special today, ladies," said Duckie, ignoring their expressions of disgust. "Let me run it by you." He raised one eyebrow and lowered his voice to a sexy croon. "How would you ladies like to be pregnant for the holidays?"

Kate hissed, "You sicko!" and slapped him across the face.

"Trouble with richies," Duckie mumbled, caressing his jaw, "no sense of adventure. Good morning, and welcome to another day of higher education," he said to Andie.

"Hi, Duckie," she said, smiling at him and shaking her head in disbelief. "How're you doing?"

Duckie held her books while she tried her lock. "Not all that bad, considering I'm in *this* dump." He checked her out. "You look volcanic today."

"Volcanic?"

"I roast for you," he said.

Andie cracked the combination on the rusty lock at last, flung open the door, and threw in her books.

"And you don't roast for me," Duckie continued.

"I don't even get warm. Sorry. Are you going to class today?"

"It crossed my mind."

"Try it, Duck. It's painless." She smiled affectionately at him. "I'll see you at lunch."

"Oh," said Duckie, "may I admire you again today?"

"If it's that important." Andie shrugged, then shook her head again. "You're outrageous. You really are. Amazing. Gotta run," she said, and did.

"I live to amuse you. Or amaze you," Duckie called after her. "Whatever turns you on." He gave her a princely bow and backed away. "Fantastic," he murmured to himself.

"Fantastic," a voice behind him agreed.

Duckie turned, but the guy who'd echoed his sentiments was heading down the hall at a good clip. All Duckie could tell from his retreating back, which was dauntingly broad, and from the button-down shirt through which an athlete's set of shoulders rippled, and the carefully creased khakis, and the butter-soft loafers without socks, and the forty-buck haircut—all he could tell was that in an us-or-them world, the dude was definitely one of *them*.

Andie was in English class, minding her own business, taking notes on a lecture so dull and dry it practically qualified as a lullabye. It was all she could do to keep her head up, her eyes open, and her pen moving.

"Culture is Matthew Arnold's most familiar catchword," Mrs. Ciccone droned, "although what he meant by it is often misunderstood."

Andie glanced over at her friend Jena and smiled. Bored to distraction, Jena was tapping a pencil to some tune playing in her head. At least, Andie thought, the lullabye Jena was listening to was accompanied by music.

She had known Jena Homan since third grade. Jena had rescued her when a tough kid named Lucille Cisco had tried to take Andie's lunch money in the schoolyard. The yard always flooded after a rain, and there were usually planks lying around, bridging the puddles. Lucille had broken a piece of wood off one of the rotting planks—a sharp, splintery piece about the size of a baseball bat. She and two other fourth graders had cornered Andie, who'd just beaten Lucille's little sister in the third-grade spelling bee.

"Okay, smartie, you better give me all your money or else," Lucille had snarled. And before Andie could say, "Oh, yeah? Make me," this scrawny eight-year-old with hair like a scarecrow's and a missing front tooth had stepped up behind Lucille and beaned her with a board.

The scrawny kid was Jena Homan. She'd just moved to Chicago from Gary, Indiana and had been in the school for exactly two days. With the odds evened up, she and Andie had taken care of Lucille's buddies together and walked away, arms around one another—Andie grinning through a nosebleed and Jena brandishing a handful of fourth-grade hair.

They'd been best friends ever since. Andie tried to catch Jena's eye now, but Jena was too spaced—oblivious to everything, even her tapping pencil.

"The term 'culture' connotes to Arnold qualities of an open-minded intelligence," Mrs. Ciccone droned on. "In this Arnold seems similar to T.H. Huxley and J.S. Mill . . ."

There was an impatient throat-clearing. Andie looked up. Benny Trombley, one of the girls who'd given her a hard time in the hall, was glaring at Jena's pencil and giving her dirty looks. Andie sighed and shook her head. She knew what was coming next. If there was anything Jena liked less than a boring lecture on Matthew Arnold, it was a richie giving her a look.

The pencil stopped tapping. Jena's middle finger went up. "Die," she mouthed.

Andie glanced quickly at Mrs. Ciccone. Jena was having a hard enough time keeping up with the classwork. All she needed to guarantee a failing grade, to kiss graduation goodbye, was to get on Ciccone's nerves: to have the English teacher accuse Jena, as just about every other teacher in the school had, of disrupting her class.

But Mrs. Ciccone hadn't noticed. Yet.

Benny glared at Jena. "Pig!" she whispered loudly. Then she flounced around in her seat and saw Andie looking at her. "May I help you?" she hissed, narrowing her eyes.

Chessy Edwards, one of Benny's crowd, gave a witchy laugh.

"Just leave her alone," Andie whispered to Benny.

"Oh, really?" Benny said.

Kate Hanson, Benny's best friend, hissed, too loudly, "Oh, God, zoid loyalty. How touching. I didn't even know zoids *had* loyalty."

"Oh, sure," Benny said, "but it's secondhand."

"*What* is secondhand, Miss Trombley?" Mrs. Ciccone stopped her lecture and turned to Benny and Kate. "And you, Miss Hanson. Is something bothering you ladies?" she asked icily.

16

Caught, they straightened up and shook their heads. Mrs. Ciccone wasn't satisfied. "Andie? Is there something going on between you and these ladies?"

Chessy Edwards and Sarah Beth Phelps sniggered. Andie decided to ignore them. She *always* decided to ignore them. Sometimes it actually worked. And sometimes her cheeks would betray her and blaze with red blotches of rage or embarrassment. Or both.

Now, Andie shook her head. "Nothing's going on that I'm aware of," she said, trying to sound matter-of-fact.

"Miss Trombley, Miss Hanson," Mrs. Ciccone began angrily.

Andie sank down in her seat. "Just shut up, lady," she whispered to herself. "*Please.*" Her face was growing warm.

But Mrs. Ciccone looked right at her. "I want to apologize on behalf of my class," she announced.

Jena groaned. Andie nodded, wishing she could disappear. She felt the heat rising in her cheeks and knew the dread blotches were back.

"Ms. Trombley and Ms. Hanson will be thinking of you this weekend," Mrs. Ciccone said significantly, glancing down at the textbook on her desk, "as they begin to write a five-hundred-word analysis of Matthew Arnold's 'Lines Written in Kensington Gardens.'"

Benny and Kate froze. The silence in the class was cold and complete. It took everything

Andie had to keep her hand from shaking as she raised it.

"Don't bother with 'Lines Written in Kensington Gardens.' Don't worry about it. Everything's cool," she said quickly. She glanced across at the girls.

Benny narrowed her eyes at Andie. Then she raised her hand. "We'll take the 'Lines Written In Kensington Gardens,' Mrs. Ciccone," she said, throwing Andie an icy smile.

Andie shook her head, narrowed her own eyes, and returned the frosty look.

"School good?" she remembered her father asking this morning.

Then he'd asked whether she was going to the Prom.

The Prom?

The Prom was the exclusive playground of the Lakefront gods and goddesses, the Sara Beths and Chessys, the Bennys and Kates.

You wouldn't catch a zoid at the Prom, any more than you'd catch a richie in the schoolyard during breaks. The fenced-in schoolyard was the zoid reservation. And the ballroom of the Biltmore on Prom night belonged exclusively to the richie tribe—the girls with the pearls and the boys with the bucks.

Three

Steff McKee was leaning against his new but already battered Porsche 944, waiting for her.

"Give me a break," Andie grumbled to herself. Her heart sank as she crossed the parking lot. If there was one thing she didn't need today, it was another run-in with a richie, another well-planned "casual encounter" with the arrogant leader of the Lakefront brat pack.

But there was Steff McKee—windblown blond hair, wrinkled gray linen jacket, white shirt opened at the collar; the tan he'd primed with skiing and burnished in Palm Beach was still rich and glowing. He was waiting for her, and there was nothing Andie could do about it. His Porsche was parked right next to her old Kharman Ghia.

There were only a few weeks left before graduation. Andie figured Steff must be getting desperate. Why else would he be waiting for her right out in the open, with nothing to hide behind but his designer shades? After all, here she was—one of the only girls in school McKee had hit upon and missed. Not that anyone knew

Steff McKee wanted Andie Walsh. No way. Mr.
Cool 'n' Casual would have cut his AmEx Gold
Card before he'd let one of his own crowd know
he had lust in his heart for anything that lived
that far west of the Lake.

"We graduate in a month, Andie," he said,
as she rifled her bag for her car keys.

Silently she looked across her car at him.

"When are you and me going to get together
and do something?"

"How about never?" Andie asked. She
jammed the key into her door lock.

Steff lowered his sunglasses and looked at
her over the tops of them. "Hey, I'm talking
more than sex," he said as if she'd hurt his
feelings.

"No, you're not."

"I've liked you for four years and you treat
me like this. What's the problem?"

"No problem."

"Listen," Steff said, strolling around the
front of the car. "I've been out with a lot of girls
at this school, babe. What makes you so different?"

"I have some taste," Andie said.

Steff stiffened. Then smiled. "That's cute.
Look, I'm not going to ask you again."

"I'd appreciate that."

Steff put his arm up on the roof of her car
and leaned casually against her door, blocking
it. His smile faded. "Nobody talks to me like
that and gets away with it, babe," he said softly.

Andie glared at him. "I've got to get to work. Move," she said. "Get out of my way."

"You're in trouble," Steff said.

Andie tugged at the car door. Lazily, Steff lifted himself off it. "You're cold, babe. Real cold."

"You should see a doctor," she answered, pulling open the door. "You have a major problem."

Steff pointed his finger at her as if it were the muzzle of a gun. "Bang," he muttered grimly as she started up the Kharman Ghia. "You're dead, babes. Big trouble."

Glad for the first time that her exhaust pipe was clogged, Andie drove away, leaving Steff McKee in a cloud of black fumes.

The music from the speakers outside Trax was blaring into the landscaped mall. Andie hurried into the record store. "New haircut, Iona?" she shouted to the slim and cynical ex-flower child who was her boss.

Iona Norman, who had the best hearing and worst taste in men Andie had ever known, shook her head—which set her new, stiff, spiked tresses trembling like extraterrestrial antennae. "New man," she called out, confirming Andie's fear. "Well, not *that* new. Couple of weeks now."

Andie hurried behind the register to ring up a sale. "Nice," she called to Iona, taking down the volume on the speakers a notch. The haircut, she meant.

Two little girls, half her age, had piled about sixty dollars' worth of tapes on the counter. Now they were going through their stonewashed jeans and fashionable leather jackets, hunting for their money. Andie smiled and shook her head as they pooled their resources— a folded fifty and a handful of balled-up tens and twenties they'd carelessly stuffed in their back pockets.

"Nice? What's nice about it?" Iona asked, artfully arranging the album flats on a display table. "I found me another heavy metal loser. Another tapped-out hippy whose claim to fame is that he would've played Woodstock if his band bus hadn't gotten rerouted in the traffic jam. Is this any way to enter middle age?"

Andie laughed and rang up the girls' sale. She loaded the tapes in two Trax shopping bags and handed them across the counter.

Iona stepped back to admire the display she'd created. "Is that classy or what?"

"It's great," Andie agreed.

"You know, I'm very good at this." Iona clicked her tongue. "It's such a waste that I have to run a lowly little retail outlet."

"Not if you're good at it," Andie said. And Iona was. Despite the costumes and hairstyles that changed with the flaky men in her life—the ones she claimed got caught in the revolving door she'd put on her bedroom—despite her brash mouth and brassy manner, Iona was a practical and dependable business person. She ran Trax a lot better than she ran her personal life. The store flourished, but Iona's ego, completely tied to romance, was always on the verge of bankruptcy.

"Hey, I'm a great cook, too," Iona cracked. "Doesn't mean I wanna make a living at it." She looked out the store window at Magique, the elegant boutique across the way. "Getting to be that time of year."

"What time?"

"Prom time. Look at 'em, window shopping, drooling over the taffeta and tulle."

Andie looked. She saw the trio of pastel ballgowns in one window of Magique and an ice-blue satin strapless alone in the other window—sophisticated, exquisite, expensive beyond her imagining. Like the store itself: carpeted in white, furnished in Victorian innocence, trimmed with pastel satin ribbons and gilt-encrusted white brocade. She'd always wanted to stop into Magique; wanted to browse along its gilded racks; wanted to feel the rich fabrics and savor the fine tailoring of the boutique's beautiful costumes. Of course she'd never dared. No one she'd ever seen pass through Magique's sleek and silent automatic double doors had looked like less than a Lakefront million.

"Did you go to your prom?" Andie asked Iona. It was an incredible thought.

"Yeah, sure." Iona adjusted her fringed hip-belt and tugged at the hem of her tight-fitting black miniskirt.

"Was it terrible?"

"The pits," Iona said, after a thoughtful pause. "That's what it's supposed to be. But you have to go, right?"

Andie shrugged.

"Oh, yeah, you have to," Iona answered her own question. "It's as much a part of the young female experience as cramps, and about as much fun. But I went. And I don't regret it, I guess. You going to yours?"

"I'm not sure," Andie said, to her own surprise. What was she talking about? Not sure? How sure did she need to be? The Prom was about two weeks away. No one she knew was going. Jena wasn't; she wouldn't be caught dead in a prom gown. And Andie could just imagine Jena's boyfriend Simon, with his foot-high spiked hair and five earrings on one lobe, slam-dancing in a dinner jacket.

"You should," Iona suddenly decided. "The memories are good. And, hey, you'll need them when you grow up and your life turns to Alpo, baby." She laughed and winked at Andie. Then, abruptly, she grabbed the staple gun off the counter, whirled around—mesh-stockinged legs planted like Dirty Harry's—and fired off a round.

A thirteen-year-old kid yowled in pain. His hand was still poised to pull an album cover from the display Iona had just put up. "Hey, whaddya—crazy?" the boy hollered, rubbing his cheek.

"I spent an hour putting that up," Iona said

without batting an eye. "I don't need you screwing with it!"

"You missed my eye by an inch!"

"I wasn't warmed up," Iona snarled. The staple gun was still aimed at the kid.

"You wouldn't!" he screamed as he took off for the door, nearly knocking over the guy who was just ambling in.

It was a tall, good-looking boy in a wrinkled buttondown shirt and clean chinos. He had a sturdy athlete's body and a shy smile. He jumped back as the kid passed him. Then, recouping his composure, he glanced sheepishly at Andie.

She looked up—and his smile wavered. She smiled at him. His breath caught. He had to look away.

Andie blinked. As if sensing it, the boy turned to her again. And tried to smile again. But she met his gaze again, and he couldn't handle it. He couldn't look at her and smile, too. He could only try to hold her eyes with his.

Blane McDonough shivered involuntarily. Iona laid the staple gun back onto the counter. "Sorry," she said to Andie. "So, when's your prom?"

Distracted, Andie blinked herself back to reality. "Uh, a couple of weeks," she said. She was watching the boy moving to the record bins.

"Are you going?" Iona asked.

"I'm not sure," Andie said, trying to focus on what she was saying. She knew the boy.

She'd seen him—where? At school? At the club she sometimes went to? No, not at Cats—never there. Cats was a pretty freaky club, and this guy was a richie. Clearly. The clothes, the clean, sandy hair that he tossed back from his fore- head, loafers without socks—definitely. At school, then. It must've been. "Most of the guys I know wouldn't touch it," she explained to Iona.

"Oh, yeah," Iona said. "I know where that one's parked. My boyfriend flat-out refused to take me. I had to go with a friend of my brother's." She thought about it for a moment. "Nice guy. Not bad-looking." She thought again. "He was twenty-six."

The telephone rang. Iona took it and walked behind the counter. Andie glanced up at the boy again. Yes, she'd seen him at school, she thought. And suddenly she knew his name, or thought she did. Blair, or was it Blane? A funny name.

"Hello, Trax. Over-priced Top Forty trash," Iona was saying into the phone. "May I help you?"

Blane. That was it. Blane McDonough! Andie had heard someone, one of the richies, talking about a guy named Blane McDonough. She'd thought, typical richie name, Blane. And then she'd seen the girl—who? Kate? Benny? one of that crowd—she'd seen her walking with him and thought, that must be the one named Blane. And sure enough, the girl had said, "Oh, come on, Blane," in that whiny, richie voice. "Oh, *Blane*, you promised."

"Yeah, right," Iona was saying wearily. "Come on, Tyrone, gimme a break. I'm working. Leave me alone."

Blane McDonough had picked out a record. He was bringing it over to the counter. Andie grabbed a quick look at her reflection in a compact disc case and brushed away a stray eyelash.

"That's thrilling," Iona drawled. "I cook for you, I do your laundry, I lend you money and you call me 'cause you need a ride to work? Why don't you grow up!" Blane stepped up to the counter.

Andie brushed back her hair and turned toward him, trying to make it seem as if she hadn't seen him approaching. She smiled what she hoped would be a nice, normal, average, unmistakably run-of-the-mill smile. He saw it, and his own grin began to waver again. He looked very nervous. And again their eyes locked.

Finally he cleared his throat. "How's it going?"

"Fine."

"That's good," he said. And the conversation died.

"Listen, you moron," Iona hissed suddenly.

Blane looked over at her. Iona smiled, shrugged, covered the mouthpiece of the phone. "Walter Mondale," she told him, and turned away again.

"You need some help?" Andie said at last.

"Yeah, as a matter of fact. Yeah, I do," he said nervously.

Andie smiled.

"Can I get your opinion on something?" Blane asked seriously.

"Maybe."

He handed her the album he'd chosen. "Is this any good?"

She looked at it. Looked back up at him. "Steve Lawrence?"

"Yeah," he said earnestly.

Andie turned the album over and pretended to be studying the jacket notes. Then she looked up at him again. He was grinning. "Oh, yeah," she said, without cracking a smile. "It's hot. White-hot."

"Great. I'll take it."

"Right," said Andie. "Cash or charge?" And, fluttering her lashes lightly, she added, "American Express Platinum Card?"

She'd nailed him. Blane smiled sheepishly. "Cash," he said, and pulled a ten out of his wallet. She took it. He held it. She pulled it free, rang up the sale, handed him his change, and bagged the record.

"Thanks for your help," he said.

Andie handed him the record. "Enjoy it."

"I'm sure I will." Blane gave her a smile and backed away from the counter. She returned his smile. Then she turned away and didn't look in his direction again until she heard the store door close behind him.

"Oh, forget it, Tyrone," Iona concluded her

call. "Look, we'll talk tonight. I'm busy making a living." Then, grudgingly, she made a kissing noise into the phone and hung up.

"Don't live past thirty, Andie," said Iona wearily. "Love turns into work and work turns into torture and torture turns into love and so on. I'm going out for a smoke."

Andie was staring at the door. "You all right?" Iona asked.

"Sure. Why?"

"I don't know. You look like somebody just soul-kissed your heart, you know?"

"I'm fine," Andie said.

"You're all red in the face."

Andie put her hands over her blazing cheeks.

"You don't have to hide it," Iona said kindly.

"I'm not hiding anything!"

"He's pretty cute."

Andie dropped her hands into her lap and sighed. "You think so?" she asked gratefully.

"Yeah. And I think he thinks you're pretty far out, too," Iona said on her way out.

Andie watched her leave. Then she stared at the door. "No way," she murmured.

Four

It was two hours later. Andie had just gotten off work. The note her father had left on the kitchen table told her that he'd gone to the employment office today, the way she'd wanted him to, and that the counselor there thought she could scare something up for him pretty soon. "Got another driving job for tonight. I'll be home late. Left you a little something over the sink," he'd written.

Andie opened the cabinet above the sink. There was a worn five-dollar bill. He'd left her some spending money.

A wave of love and pity washed over her. Jack had been an ironworker for thirty years, on and off. And a bum for five. That was how he looked at it, how he always put it. He hadn't just been an ironworker, either; he'd been an ornamental ironworker, which he said had turned out to mean last hired, first fired in a crunch. And the crunch had come from every direction five years ago.

First Andie's mother had walked out. Andie had been thirteen years old. She'd come home from school and found the note on the

kitchen table. Catherine Walsh had written it on
the back of a brown paper bag. Four words. "I
hope you're satisfied."

She must have known what it meant, because she remembered how her throat had
tightened and tears had sprung to her eyes and
how suddenly she'd been barely able to breathe
for the pain in her chest—heartache, she'd
always thought, that's what heartache felt like.

Panting, still clutching her books to her
chest, Andie had gone into her parents' room.
Sure enough, the closet doors were open and
the dresser drawers were pulled out and just
about everything that had belonged to her
mother was gone. What was left—on the floor
next to an empty pack of her mother's cigarettes—were a couple of old letters, some snapshots, a piece of pink ribbon, and a squashed-
flat rose.

Andie had knelt and picked up one of the
snapshots. A torn one. It hadn't mattered to her
right then what was left of the snapshot, only
that half of it was gone. She'd slipped the
picture quickly into her pocket. And then she'd
gone back to the kitchen and sat at the table
waiting for her father to come home.

He'd walked in, tall and smiling, unsus-
pecting. He was wearing his heavy workboots, a
clean pair of pants, a sweet-smelling, ironed
shirt, and his big old plaid wool jacket. He had a
paperback book in his jacket pocket; his overalls and workshirt were rolled up under one

arm, and a six-pack in a brown paper sack was under the other.

Her father saw that Andie had been crying. He read the note. He ran into the bedroom. And when he came back out, his face was ashy white. His eyes were red. It looked as though he'd entered an evil magician's castle: he'd gone in a regular man and come out gray and old, with all the laughter stolen from his soul. And that was that.

For about a week or two after that, Andie remembered, her father would come home from work, leave her a sandwich and a soft drink he'd picked up at the deli, fix a thermos of coffee for himself, and leave again. He'd just get in his car early every evening and drive off. Usually he didn't get home until morning. Whether he was out looking for her mother or just driving, Andie didn't know.

Night after night she sat out on the porch alone, shivering, waiting for her dad to come home. Then one night Duckie had stopped by.

Andie hadn't told anyone that her mother had left, not even Jena. She was too ashamed. She was afraid someone might think that she had done something terrible to drive her mother away. What else could they think? But Duckie came into the yard and sat down on the step just beneath her. And he said, "Well, he's gone again." And Andie had thought he meant her father. She'd wondered how Duckie Dale knew that Jack left home every night.

She'd looked at Duckie. She'd said, "Who told you?"

"No one had to tell me," he replied. "My mother's in there breaking dishes. She always does when he leaves."

"When who leaves?" Andie'd asked suspiciously.

"My old man," Duckie said. "He took off for Milwaukee again. Who'd you think I meant?"

"My father," said Andie. "I thought you meant my father." She'd started to laugh. Duckie joined her. Then he said, "Hey, what're we cackling about, Andie? I don't get it."

And she told him. She had to tell him. She didn't know it until she began, but she'd been hurting to tell someone. And Duckie had listened, quietly, respectfully. Listened until she got to the part where she said, "And I don't even know what I did wrong."

"Aw, Andie, come on," he'd said then, as if she were being really dumb, and she had burst into tears.

He had sat next to her quietly while she cried, and he'd only said one other thing. He'd said, "I wouldn't have, Andie. I wouldn't have left you." Then he'd gotten quiet again and just sat there, and she'd stopped feeling so icy cold. And after that she'd started to get better.

But her father never had. The weeks of driving and not sleeping and then going straight out to work left their mark on him. And one night he came home and tossed his pink slip down on the table. He'd been laid off.

For a while after that, he'd get up every morning and fix her breakfast and drive her to school. Sometimes, she'd walk into the kitchen and catch him wiping his eyes. She'd see that he'd been crying. But, for a little while, he had gotten up early and showered and shaved and, after he'd dropped her off at school, he'd gone downtown to the union halls and to the employment offices looking for work. It seemed to Andie that he thought if he got a job, her mother would find out about it some way and come back to him.

What he got was part-time work: tending bar, playing a little piano, driving a cab some nights. He didn't need to shave every day, so he stopped. And he stopped going downtown looking for real work. There wasn't a factory hiring for a hundred miles around. And Andie knew, even though he denied it, that her father would never look for work out of town. At first she'd thought it was because he expected her mother to come home. And, at first, maybe it was.

But after a while Andie began to believe it was because her father couldn't leave *her*. He was all she had, and he wasn't going to walk out on her the way her mother had, not until Andie was ready to go out on her own—which was, finally, just a few months down the road.

One of the five scholarships she'd applied for was bound to come through. Her teachers said so. Her guidance counselor said so. Her Art and Design teacher had written glowing letters of recommendation for her to the top fashion schools in the east. It was just a matter of time.

Andie looked at her watch. She was late. She'd promised Jena and Simon that she'd meet them at the club the way she always did on Friday nights—and here she was, standing in the kitchen, daydreaming. She took the five-dollar bill her father had left for her and carried it into his room. She put the money in the pocket of his favorite jacket, where she knew he'd come across it in a few days' time and be amazed at his good fortune. For good measure, she crumpled two more five-dollar bills. She dropped one into one of his Sunday shoes and put the other in the back of his overalls. Then she grabbed a few spoonfuls of the chili he'd left on the stove for her, showered, changed, fed the dog, hopped back into the noisy Kharman Ghia, and took off for Cats.

Jena and Simon were already at the club. Andie found them sitting at a tiny table behind the dingy dance floor. They had four empty glasses in front of them. There was a lime rind on the table, too, as well as a pyramid of soft-drink cans and a bracelet made of metal can tabs. In the deafening noise and dim light, Jena was putting polish on her nails. It looked black, but Andie couldn't tell. Simon, his combat boots spit-shined, his hair at attention, was sucking on a plastic straw.

The music was blaring. Jena waggled her

wet nails at Andie across the table, then leaned over and kissed her cheek. "Did you believe Ciccone today? Give me a break!" she hollered.

"You owe me," Andie shouted back.

"Right," said Jena, winking. "See my lawyer." She tossed her head at Simon, who was staring silently at Andie, without expression. At least, Andie thought he was staring at her. It might have been the people behind her he was watching, or the wall behind the people, for that matter. Simon usually stared vacantly into space.

"Dance?" one of the regulars asked Andie. She hung her purse around Simon's neck and followed the boy onto the dance floor. Three songs later she returned, flushed and sweaty. Her purse was still hanging around Simon's neck. She lifted it carefully over his spiky hair. "Thanks," she said.

"Whuffor?" said Simon, blinking at her.

"Holding my bag, you know."

"Oh," he said. Then he was silent again. And then, "Oh, that," he said, and thought about it and nodded a couple of times. As Andie slid into the seat next to Jena, Simon said, "No problem."

Jean shook her head at the exchange. "Some things never change," she said.

Andie laughed. "Been here long?"

"All night," Jena said.

"Some things never change," said Simon, without looking at either of them.

Jena and Andie cracked up. "Nice timing!" Andie said.

"Yeah," said Simon, gazing over their heads.

"So how's it going?" Andie asked Jena.

"A notch above survival. You?"

"Some things never change," Andie said. She picked a couple of pieces of ice out of one of the glasses and chewed on them for a minute. "Jena . . ." she said, staring at the dance floor.

"Yeah?" Jena was looking out at the dancers, too.

"Would you ever go out with somebody who had money?"

Jena turned slowly and stared at her.

"No?" Andie said.

Jena didn't blink. "Do sheep wear sweaters?"

"Somebody can't help being born with money any more than somebody can help being born . . . without."

Jena tilted her head and studied Andie silently.

"Simon?" Andie asked, turning away from Jena's scrutiny. "What would you do if your father was loaded?"

Without hesitation, Simon said: "Anything he wanted."

Andie glanced at Jena. She was still staring. "See?" Andie said.

"See what?"

"What Simon said."

"What are you getting at, Andie? Are you going out with a richie or something?"

"Me? You think I'm . . ." Andie didn't even finish the sentence. She just shrugged and rolled her eyes to show how absurd she thought the question was.

"Are you fantasizing about one?"

"Fantasizing?" Andie asked, as if she wasn't sure she'd heard correctly.

"Wishing?" Jena persisted.

Andie looked at her watch. "I gotta split," she said, although she couldn't even see the dial in the smoky half-light.

"You didn't answer my question."

"Simon," Andie said, ignoring Jena, "it's been stimulating." She grabbed her purse and slid out of her chair.

"Yeah," said Simon.

"Andie? You're kidding, right?"

Andie hesitated. Then she smiled.

"I knew it. Thank God," said Jena. She sounded relieved.

Duckie Dale was waiting outside Cats. It was Friday night, and the Duck Man was ready to party. He slid his palm along the cresting wave of his hair.

"How long have I been coming down here, Jimbo?" he asked the club's huge bouncer. They were sitting side by side on beat-up folding chairs outside the entrance to the bar.

"Couple years," Jimbo Jamkarnsi said.

"We're buddies, right?" Duckie offered the bouncer his bag of potato chips.

"Yeah," said Jimbo in a bored voice, foraging for a perfect chip. "I guess so."

"Okay. How many times have you let me in?" Duckie asked.

The bouncer's brow, which had been furrowed with concentration, smoothed as he plucked a large, flawless, nearly translucent chip from Duckie's bag and studied it with pleasure. "I never let you in," he said.

"That's what I'm getting at, Jimbo. My eighteenth birthday's a mere half year away. My girlfriend's in there. And I'm out here. You're a sensitive guy. You have to know how that hurts."

"How come she comes here when she knows I don't let you in?" Jimbo asked.

Duckie shot the cuffs of his shiny pink-on-pink shirt, then adjusted his skinny tie. "I don't know. It's a mystery to me. But how can a guy expect to enjoy a fruitful relationship with a lady when he can't accompany her to her favorite watering hole?"

"Love hurts," the bouncer said, polishing the chip off in a single bite.

"That's the plain truth, bro'." Duckie held his hand up, and Jimbo gave it a soul slap. Behind them, the club door opened and Andie stepped out. She saw Duckie sitting alongside the huge bouncer. She walked over and stopped behind him.

"You go for one lady at a time, huh?" Jimbo was saying.

"Basically," Duckie confided. He smoothed back his hair again. "Multiple relations get too confusing. I mean, it's embarrassing waking up in some broad's penthouse and not remembering her name."

Andie rolled her eyes. "Hi, Duckie," she said. She walked past him toward her car.

Duckie froze. "I been caught bad, buddy," he groaned. He threw the bag of potato chips into Jimbo's lap and scrambled to his feet. "Gotta run," he called over his shoulder.

He caught up to her halfway across the parking lot, and his face lit up the way it always did when he saw her. "Hi, Andie. What I was saying back there—" he began.

Andie looked at him with a barely suppressed smile. Duckie cleared his throat. "Total invention," he said. "Jimbo's pretty thick, you know? He buys anything I say."

"Were you out here long?"

"Nah. Three, four hours." He shrugged. What was three, four hours between friends? "Have a good time?" Duckie asked, slowing his loping gait to walk beside her.

She nodded.

"What now?" he asked, clapping his hands together with a burst of enthusiasm.

"Bed," Andie said.

Duckie chuckled. "Yours or mine?"

Andie stared at him.

"Ours?" he asked lamely.

"Nice try." Andie laughed and walked on ahead to her car. Duckie hurried after her.

"Can you give me a lift home?"

She nodded and took out her car keys.

"Can I put my head in your lap?"

Ignoring him, she unlocked the car door.

"Can I rest it on your shoulder and help you steer?"

Andie got into her car, reached over, and unlocked Duckie's door. He pulled it open. "Andie, I'm kidding," he said, softly, without looking at her. "I only do this because I know it'll never happen. It's a joke," he said somberly. Then he sighed and got into the car and closed the door. "One kiss?" he asked, grinning again.

Andie started up the motor.

"Is this too sad?" He laid his head on her shoulder and blinked like an unhappy clown. "Too desperate?"

She patted his head and shrugged him off. If Duckie's feelings were hurt, he didn't show it. He sat up with new enthusiasm and snapped on the cassette deck as she headed east.

It took him a while to realize they were driving out toward the lake. "Hey, I thought we were going home!" he said. "What're we doing here, scouting locations for 'Lifestyles of the Rich and Famous'?"

Andie began cruising along broad tree-lined avenues bordered by protective gates and sweeping manicured lawns. "Can you imagine what it must be like to live in a house that big?"

she asked, gazing at the turrets of a sprawling Tudor mansion.

"No," said Duckie. "I'm limited." He took out the tape he'd started and inserted a new one.

Andie drove slowly, looking out at the magnificent houses, while Duckie toyed with the cassette player. No song seemed to satisfy him. He'd let each play for about three beats before fast-forwarding the tape.

"Aren't these houses amazing, Duck?"

"First million I make," he said, "I'll buy you one. I hate this song."

"They're so beautiful."

"You want beauty, look in the mirror." The tape squealed violently as he hit the fast-forward again. "This tape is horrible!" He took it out and searched for another. "I must be going through a hormone thing. Every song I listen to makes me sick. Why can't I find a decent song?" He slipped another tape into the cassette deck and hit Play.

Andie pulled over to the curb and stopped. Next to them was a magnificent house at the crest of a circular driveway, far back on a landscaped stretch of lawn. "That one's my favorite," she said.

"Are you deaf?" Duckie asked, thinking she meant the song.

"The house, Duck."

"Oh," he said, looking out the window at last. "Nice little crib. God, this neighborhood's so quiet! It knocks me out. It's like the Rollses and Mercedes are all asleep, you know, tucked into their little garages. Oh, wow, Andie, look, there's a BMW that's been put out for the night. What a place—hey, babe, take a walk on the *mild* side." He returned to his music. "I'm yearning for a good ballad."

"I wonder what it's like inside," Andie murmured, still gazing at the house.

"What difference does it make?"

"None. I just think it's pretty."

"Yeah, but I'll bet the guy that owns it doesn't think it's so pretty when he has to cut the grass," said Duckie.

Andie stared at him.

"It's got to be an all-day affair," he explained.

"At *least*," Andie said, shaking her head at him. "The sad thing is, the people who live there probably just take it for granted. They probably don't think it's half as beautiful as I do."

"Probably," said Duckie, after considering her point. "But you don't have to cut the grass."

Andie gave up. She began to say something, then changed her mind and gave him a half-smile. Then she started the car up again.

"You know, Andie? It's true," he said, as she drove away. "They don't write love songs like they used to."

Five

Monday morning. Andie hit the alarm clock and slid one foot to the floor. Her eyes felt impossibly heavy. Just before she opened them, a fragment of the dream she'd been having came back to her.

The boy had said to her mother, "She'll be fine. Don't you worry, Mrs. Walsh." They were walking together to his car, which was waiting at the end of the circular driveway. She was wearing a pink prom gown. He was wearing a tuxedo and brown leather loafers with no socks. As he held open the car door for her, she glanced back at the house. Standing between the sparkling white pillars flanking the entrance were her parents. Her beautiful mother was crying. Her father was trying to comfort her. He had his arm around her waist. His pale hand clutched the pink satin sash of her gown. "She'll be fine, Catherine," Andie could hear him saying. She waved to them and turned to get into the car.

But when she looked down, the boy wasn't wearing brown leather loafers anymore. He had enormous feet, and he was wearing a pair of huge hightop sneakers. The last thing she remembered was her mother's voice. She was speaking as if she really meant it—speaking without a trace of meanness or sarcasm and saying, in the saddest, sweetest, lovingest voice Andie had ever heard: "I hope you're satisfied."

Andie opened her eyes slowly and slid her other foot to the floor. She sat up, and the first thing she saw was the portrait of her mother on the table beside her bed.

It wasn't that she actually *saw* the picture of her mother. What she saw was that it was still there. It had been in its oval frame on her bedside table since before her mother left. Andie had never moved it. She'd never touched it. In fact, she rarely looked at it at all. And this morning was no exception—except that this morning, for the first time, she found herself thinking about the fact that there was a portrait of her mother next to her bed, and that it was her real mother—the mother she had known and still remembered, not the pink prom girl whose snapshot was stuck in her dresser mirror. It was the prom girl she always dreamed about; never the mother who had left her. Never, until last night, or this morning, or whenever it was that the mother in her dream had said, "I hope you're satisfied."

Andie looked across the room to the dresser mirror and squinted at the torn snapshot of the girl in the pink gown—the beautiful fairy godmother who had been left to protect her, to stand guard over her until . . . Until what? Until her real mother returned?

She wasn't coming back. Not ever. Andie had known that from the beginning. Her real mother, Catherine Mary Walsh, had packed her bags and taken everything with her. Everything except a handful of fading souvenirs, among them the pressed rose that came alive in Andie's dreams and the torn photograph that she loved.

She stood up lazily and stretched and yawned. And the thought came into her slowly waking mind that the girl in the pink prom gown would never have said, "I hope you're satisfied." But the mother in her dream had.

It dawned on her that for the very first time she had allowed her mother's voice into her dreams. And the voice had not been icy or angry or mean.

Monday afternoon. Andie went to the school library to do research on her social studies paper. She found an empty cubicle, slid into the seat in front of the computer console, and punched in her request for information from the source bank.

She opened her notebook. As she fished around in her bag for a pencil, the data she wanted began to come up on the screen:

More than 8,500,000 men and women were employed in building and improvement jobs, and . . .

She was copying down the statistics when suddenly her source feed was interrupted. A new message—a pirate message—appeared on her screen:

Do you want to talk?

Andie rolled her eyes, sighed, and tapped out her reply:

Duckie, I'm working.

A moment later, another message came up:

Who's Duckie?

Who's Duckie? Exasperated, Andie stood up and peered over the top of her cubicle. All she could see were other cubicles and the heads of students intently bent toward their screens. In fact, even on tiptoes, she could see only the tops of the bent heads, and not one of them had slicked-back high black hair. And not one of them was wearing a snap-brim hat.

Well, if it wasn't Duckie jamming her computer, who was it? Jena wouldn't be caught dead in the school library. She probably didn't even know where the library was. Simon probably didn't know *what* it was. Baffled, Andie settled back into her seat. And another message appeared:

I'm waiting.

She cocked her head at the screen. She looked over her shoulder. It had to be some chip-head fooling around, and he'd obviously cut into the wrong computer. She entered a message of her own:

Do you know who I am?

There was nothing for a moment. Then a digitized picture began to come up. It was a yearbook photo. Of her! Dumbfounded, she stared at the portrait of Andie Walsh staring at her from the computer screen, and tried again to figure out what was happening. Finally she keyed in:

Do you know who you are?

A moment passed. The screen unloaded. And a new digitized photo came up. Andie squinted at it. It was him! Blane. He was the boy in her dream, she realized suddenly, the one who'd worn the tuxedo. She was looking at Blane McDonough's yearbook picture.

Andie stood up again, slowly. She inched up out of her seat and peered cautiously over the top of her cubicle. The boy was standing up slowly too, peering cautiously over the top of the cubicle facing hers.

She gasped. Then she laughed. Then she just looked at him.

Blane McDonough smiled.

Six

On Wednesday morning, Andie's father wet down his hair, put on his favorite jacket, and took a bus downtown to the employment office. Mrs. Burson, the woman he'd seen there the week before, had phoned on Monday to say she thought she might have something for him. What with one thing and another, he hadn't gotten around to seeing her until Wednesday. Of course, the job was gone by then.

But in the elevator, he'd thrust his hands forlornly into his jacket pockets and had found a five-dollar bill. Jack fingered it now, on his way out of the building. Two feet to the left was the bus for home. Two doors to the right was the bar where he'd put away a few too many after his first appointment with the employment counselor.

That first visit. She'd scared the daylights out of him. She'd looked and acted like every schoolteacher who'd ever threatened to fail him. She'd sat squinting down at her papers, pencil poised, asking personal questions in that schoolteacher voice that had made him feel like he'd better come up with the right answers or else.

She'd said, "Well, what have you been getting by on?"

"I do a little part-time work. Tend bar, drive a cab when I can. I play piano sometimes. I'm happy with it. It gets me by. The house is paid off, my daughter works. You want to know how often I shave and what I read in the john?"

Mrs. Burson rattled her papers and said, "You probably shave when you come here, and I imagine you read the sports section."

"Actually, I'm reading James Joyce right now. *Finnegan's Wake*."

Nothing. She stared at him for a minute, then continued the interrogation.

"You're divorced?"

He said, "Not officially."

She put down her pencil, folded her hands, and gave him a long sigh.

"My wife Catherine left us four, five years back," he said, reaching for a cigarette. Right behind Mrs. Burson's head was a No Smoking sign, but without even thinking he just pulled one out and lit up. "I don't know from day to day where she is," he said, "so a divorce hasn't been particularly convenient."

To her credit, the counselor hadn't said a word about the cigarette, the No Smoking sign, the smoke ring he'd blown past her ear, or the fact that he'd had to dump his ashes in his cuff. She'd said she'd see what she could find for him in the way of fulltime work.

After that, he'd headed for the bar downstairs. And he'd given Catherine a kind of burial at sea. Said goodbye, dumped her overboard, and drowned his sorrow, all in the same ocean of whiskey.

It hadn't been so bad today, though. Jack Walsh looked at the five-dollar bill in his hand and thought of what he and the counselor had just finished talking about.

She'd said it didn't look to her as though he was serious about finding work—seeing how he'd shown up two days late for a job interview.

He'd said, she could bet he *was* serious about it. Didn't he have a daughter to support? Didn't she think he was serious about that? He'd been doing it, doing the best he could all alone for five years now. It was only getting laid off that had messed him up so.

And then, for no good reason he could think of—she was such a sour-faced biddy— Jack had started telling Mrs. Burson about how he'd driven all over the country after Catherine had left. Night after night, literally driven himself nuts. He'd just gone to pieces when Catherine walked out on them. Five years ago. Andie was just thirteen.

"I've been feeling sorry for myself and disgusted with the world for about that long," he admitted to her. "Only now, it's Andie I feel sorry for, and myself I'm disgusted with."

And he meant to change. He'd never talked about it before. Not ever. But today he'd told this stranger.

Mrs. Burson had asked him about Andie, then, and he nearly burst with pride describing his daughter to her. He'd pull the fiver out of his jacket pocket. "I know it was my daughter who put it there," he told the counselor. "There can't be two fives as worn out as that one in the whole state." He told her how he'd left it for Andie and she'd sneaked it back into his pocket, thinking he was so out of it he'd never put two and two together and come up with four.

Burson had smiled! She'd never done that before. Neither had he, come to think of it. So they'd sat there—Jack Walsh, stiff-necked with pride, and the lady who was trying to find steady work for him. They sat across the desk from each other, grinning like good old friends. She promised she'd look long and hard and she'd find something for him. And he promised he'd show up for the interview, bright-eyed and bushy-tailed, whenever and wherever she said.

Jack Walsh went into the bar, broke the five for bus fare, and walked out again, sober and dry. Then he went home and started cleaning up the yard.

"You puttin' the place up for sale?" Duckie Dale asked, strolling through the rickety front gate.

"Spring cleaning," Jack said, mopping his brow. "And I'm just about done. Andie's not home. She's over working at the record shop."

"Yeah, I know. Can I get you a beer?"

"Sure," Jack said, rolling down the sleeves of his workshirt. "Sounds good to me. Take yourself one, too."

Duckie loped into the house. He came out drinking a box of juice and carrying a six-pack of beer. Jack opened a couple of rusty lawn chairs, and they sat down in the yard together on the new, short-cropped patches of dry grass. Alongside the house was a plastic bag filled with empty beer cans and the tires, jacks, nuts, bolts, springs, and hubcaps that, half-hidden by tall weeds, had once littered the yard.

"The lawn looks great," said Duckie. "I wish I'd gotten here earlier so I could have helped you out."

"Thanks," Jack said, "but I needed the exercise."

"Cardiovascular type thing?"

Jack raised an eyebrow. "Whatever."

"It's good exercise. I had a landscaping business back in the sixth grade. Ran it for a couple months, then sold out to fifth-graders."

"How're your folks?" Jack asked.

Looking away uncomfortably, Duckie took a last long slurp of juice. Then he crushed the empty paper carton as though it were a beer can. "It's hard to say." He shrugged and shook his head. "They split up again."

"Sorry to hear that," Jack said.

"It's no big deal," said Duckie. "My dad went back to Milwaukee. He always goes back to Milwaukee. Probably got another family stashed there. I don't know. But he might as well. He spends more time there than with us. And since I'm not real crazy about my mom's lifestyle, I'm staying with my brother. It's cool. He doesn't give me too much crap. Pardon my French."

Jack nodded and popped open another beer.

"You know, Jack," Duckie said. "—Can I call you Jack?"

"Sure."

"You can call me Duckie."

"I do," Jack said.

"Right." Duckie stretched his legs out in front of him and crossed his ankles. "Anyway, Jack, the reason for my visit—other than that I'd been planning for some time now to drop in and see you anyway—the reason I came over is I want to talk about Andie."

Jack stopped the beer can en route to his lips and looked over at Duckie with curiosity.

"She's an incredible individual."

Beer still poised at his lips, Jack smiled.

"And I'm beholden to you for having had the foresight to create her," Duckie continued. "She's the joy of my life. Yours too, I imagine."

Jack nodded.

"I'm here for her, Jack. Whenever, however. I'm here," Duckie said with passionate conviction. "You can rest assured that she's covered. I don't want you to worry because my only future plans are to see that she's taken care of."

Jack looked Duckie over. He saw a skinny kid in clown-size sneakers and cutoff jeans, with a faded black t-shirt under a shiny, yellowish-green sharkskin sportcoat. The straw porkpie hat Duckie wore was pushed back on his head to highlight his carefully constructed wave.

"That's nice of you, Duckie," Jack said, allowing himself a good-sized gulp of beer. "Real nice."

"I'd like to marry her."

Jack's jaw dropped open.

"Not today. Eventually," Duckie quickly added, sitting up and dusting off what turned out to be a small hole in the elbow of his jacket sleeve.

"Does Andie know your plans?"

Duckie grinned and shook his head. "No confirmation on it yet. I'm laying the groundwork. I'm thinking in terms of supporting her— housing, basic needs type of stuff. I'll get that together. Then, you know, I'll lay it on her. You can understand that, can't you?"

The heartbreak of it, Jack thought, was that he could. And did. He looked at Duckie's oversized feet and then down at his own dusty workboots. It surprised him, for a moment, to see that he'd finally grown into them, those feet that used to trip him up, step on toes, mow down everything in their way. "Oh, yeah," he said kindly. "In fact, I once felt that same way about somebody."

"A girl?"

Jack took another swallow of beer. What
did the kid think he was talking about, a pet
goldfish? He smiled, and Duckie shook his head
in embarrassment.

"A girl," Jack said. "She was my everything. The sun, the moon. My every waking
breath . . ."

Duckie reached over and patted Jack's
shoulder consolingly. "You're singing my song,
Jack baby."

"That's what I'm afraid of."

"How so?"

"As far as I can tell, Duckie, love is a
natural thing. It can't be forced. You can't force
somebody to love you."

"Wow," said Duckie, nodding as if he were
impressed. "You're a very bright man, Jack.
Have you ever considered writing a book?"

The kid was listening but not hearing, Jack
knew. He sighed, took a last sip of beer, and set
down the can. "Son, listen to me. You can love
Andie, but that won't mean she'll love you. It
doesn't mean she won't, but I'm saying don't
think you can make it happen. It will or it
won't. It's all in the heart. And the heart doesn't
listen to the brain. You understand?"

"Perfectly, Jack."

"Love is strange," Jack said.

"Uh-huh," said Duckie

"You're not listening to me, Duckie."

"*Au contraire*, Jack. You're coming in loud
and clear."

Jack closed his eyes and shook his head.

Then he smiled. "What the hell, Duck!" He sighed and slapped Duckie's back. "I never listened either." He picked up the empty beer cans and carried them over to the trash bag. "I gotta go. I have an appointment with the vacuum cleaner."

Duckie stood up, too. "You're on kind of a home-improvement jag, huh?"

"Turning the old life around."

"Hey, more power to you," said Duckie. "Tina Turner did it. Jack Walsh can do it, too." He patted Jack's back. "Well," he said, "I'm off like a dirty shirt."

Seven

It was a slow afternoon at Trax. The only customer in the store was a pre-pube boy pawing through the Duran Duran albums.

Andie plucked a pair of pop sunglasses from the counter rack and tried them on. They were amazing—Dayglo-pink frames with flamingos on the the earpieces. She checked herself out in the compact disc case behind her. The glasses were a riot. She looked certifiable. She wouldn't be caught dead in them.

The store door opened. Andie turned to see who it was.

It was Blane McDonough.

Andie whipped off the dumb glasses. They sailed across the store and landed in the Country-Western bin, missing the preteen by inches. The poor kid looked up at the ceiling as if he expected to see the whimsical genie who'd dropped them.

"Hi! Hello," Andie said, laughing like a goon. She waved her hand nervously, as if her nails needed drying. "We just got those glasses in, and . . ." Blane was staring at her hand. She

58

put it behind her back. "They're really . . ." She shrugged and shook her head and rolled her eyes. "You know . . ."

Blane smiled. "I didn't like that album I got the other day."

"So dumb. Oh, God. What?"

"The album," he said. He was still having trouble looking full at her. But less trouble than last time, she noticed. "The one I bought. It was too . . ."

"Hip?" Andie suggested.

Blane brightened but kept a straight face. "Yeah," he said. "That's it. Could you recommend something a little less political?"

She smiled. "Lionel Ritchie?" she asked, moving behind the counter toward the Contemporary Pop section.

The burglar alarm went off with a piercing clamor. Andie gasped. The noise was coming from the stock room. "Ugh!" she shouted, clapping her hands over her ears and rushing toward the back of the store. "I'm here alone. Oh, God. Hold on. Please," she hollered over her shoulder.

She left Blane stunned and wide-eyed in front of the cash register and burst into the storeroom.

There was Duckie Dale, trying to look casual, leaning against the office desk. Andie screeched to a stop when she saw him.

"Hi!" Duckie yelled over the noise of the alarm. "How's it going?"

He backed quickly out of Andie's way as

she stomped up to the desk and fished a key out of the top drawer. She shot him a dirty look on her way to the alarm box. Finally she shut the alarm off.

"Wow. That baby pumps out about three hundred decibels, doesn't it?"

"Did you do this?"

"I'm not sure," said Duckie, fighting to hang onto his friendly grin in the face of her fire. "I was, uh, using your restroom and I, um, decided not to disturb you so I was going to go out the back door. I just touched it. The rest is, as they say, history—"

Blane breathed a sigh of relief as the alarm stopped ringing. He was watching the back door, waiting for Andie to return, when the front door opened and in walked Steff McKee. Steff had been cruising by with a couple of the guys, who were waiting outside Trax. John Noonan nodded at Blane through the store window. Allie Crompton punched Noonan's arm, then gave Blane a thumbs-up.

"Hey, babes, what're you doing?" Steff asked, looking around the record store.

"Nothing," Blane said. He hoped Andie wouldn't show up now. He wanted to talk to her, get to know her, and he'd never be able to do it with Steff and the guys hanging around. He didn't want to answer questions about her or make dumb jokes, which was exactly what they'd expect him to do. He didn't feel like pretending she was just some chick he had the hots for. And he knew them well enough to know that was exactly what they'd think. She wasn't one of their crowd. She was smart, beautiful, graceful, proud, and utterly unique. But all they'd see was that she was a zoid.

Steff might possibly understand. He was Blane's best friend. They'd hung out together all their lives. But Blane wasn't going to discuss it with Steff. There wasn't time right now, and Blane didn't really feel like explaining anything. Especially to Steff, who always seemed to be able to talk Blane into thinking whatever Steff wanted him to think. Blane always hated himself for giving in—but he always gave in. Maybe it was just easier that way.

"Just checking out some tunes," Blane said.

Steff looked around the store. "Yeah?" he asked, grinning skeptically. "Find anything?"

"Not really." Blane glanced at the stock-room door. Where was she? What was she doing back there? She had cut the alarm. She'd be out any second. And Steff would see her and try to figure out what was going on. And then he'd probably give Blane one of his knowing looks. He'd raise an eyebrow, maybe, or pucker his lips, or make a dumb gesture with his fist. And maybe he'd say something stupid like, "Go for it, man."

"You cut out on me after school," Steff was saying. "Any special reason?" He was grinning again—a coy, half-angry grin.

Blane put his arm around Steff's shoulder

and started for the door. "No, man," he said. "Nothing special."

Andie reset the alarm. "How'd you get back here?" she demanded.

"Are you mad?" Duckie asked.

"Yes!" It came out too loud, too mean. "Yes," she said, taking it down a notch. "I'm mad. There are public bathrooms all over the place."

"Hey, I'm not nine, Andie. I know that," Duckie said, sounding a little peevish himself. "It's the end of the month, all right? Everybody's out of toilet seat covers."

"Sometimes I can't understand you."

"I screwed up. I'm sorry. I don't have anything to do. I like coming here. Excuse me very much."

Andie sighed. "It's okay. I didn't mean to get so mad. It's okay." She smiled at him. "Listen, I have to get back out front."

She left him and went back out to the shop. It was empty. No one was there except the little kid, now pawing through the Country-Western bin. He looked up at her. He was wearing the pink sunglasses with flamingos on the earpieces.

It's 6:05. Duckie Dale. Call me. BEEP. It's 6:15. Duckie Dale. Call me. BEEP. Andie? Where are you? It's 6:45. This is Duck. Call me. BEEP. Are you okay? It's Duckie Dale. Call me. BEEP.

The last voice Andie heard that night was not the voice she wanted to hear. While the answering machine messages played back, Andie sat on her bed, staring up at the patch of evening sky visible from her window.

This is Duckie. Are you really home and just not answering? If so, I feel like a complete jerk. It's 8:30. Call me. Please.

Blane McDonough hadn't phoned. What had made her think he would? She flipped off the machine and lay back on her bed.

The phone rang. Andie reached over and picked it up. "Duckie," she said, without waiting for him to speak, "I'll talk to you in the morning." She hung up and turned off the light.

Eight

The door was closed. The music was blasting. The water was running. Andie was still in the shower.

Jack hurried down the hall to the kitchen. Ace, Andie's dog, was pawing at the screen door. Jack let him in. "Shhh," he said, finger to his lips. "Let's surprise her. What do you say?"

"Daddy! Get out of bed!" Andie called from the shower.

Jack cracked a pair of eggs into a frying pan. He prodded them gently with a spatula, then slid the spatula delicately under one egg. "Ready? Watch this," he whispered to the attentive dog. "One, two . . . three!" he said.

He flicked the spatula.

The egg flew over his shoulder and landed on the floor right in front of Ace, who polished it off in two seconds flat.

Jack looked at the dog in disgust.

Andie came into the kitchen. She was wearing a man's bathrobe and drying her hair with a Holiday Inn towel. "What're you doing up? I didn't wake you yet," she said, surprised to see him.

"I made you breakfast." He slipped the remaining egg onto a plate for her. "One egg, sunnyside up." He glanced at Ace. "And I fed the dog."

Andie walked over to the counter and started to clean up the mess he'd made.

"Your egg?"

She smiled at him. "I don't really eat eggs, Daddy. You have it." She walked him over to the table, took the plate from him, and set it down. "Go on. I'll make your coffee."

"Since when don't you like eggs?" Jack asked, pulling a chair up to the table.

"Since about birth. I never eat breakfast. Don't worry about it." She kissed the top of his head, then sniffed and grinned. "Mmmm, your hair smells so clean. You didn't tell me why you're up."

"It's morning," Jack grumbled. "You mean why you didn't have to drag me out of bed and scold me?"

She filled the coffeepot with water. "Okay."

"I have to go to work. I got a . . . job."

Smiling, Andie turned from the counter. "No!"

Her father nodded.

"Where?"

"I'm not telling you till I start."

"When's that?" Andie asked.

"Soon." He stood up and took her in his arms, and she squeezed him hard.

"I'm really proud, Daddy."

"It's no big deal, honey," Jack said sheepishly.

"Yeah, it is." Andie kissed his cheek. "I'm going to be late. You can tell me more tonight, okay?"

"All right. It's gonna be good!" he called after her enthusiastically. He watched her walk out. Then he sat back down in front of the plate and put his head in his hands. He looked at the egg. He'd lost his appetite. He glanced down at Ace. The dog snarled at him. "All right," Jack said. "So I lied."

Her father was a terrible liar. He didn't lie often; he only lied badly. Still, seeing him awake and smiling early in the morning, smelling of soap, shampoo, and aftershave instead of beer and cigarettes, had been a terrific surprise. So terrific it almost made up for Blane McDonough's disappearing act yesterday. Now you see him, now you don't, Andie thought, as she sat on a bench in the school courtyard, sketching and eating her lunch.

The noon courtyard was filled with freaks, motorheads, metalheads, and assorted misfits. It was from their varied and colorful outfits that Andie drew inspiration for her designs. Even the lowliest zoid had a unique sense of style. It was, Andie thought, the fact that they dressed as individuals and didn't wear the same bland clothes their parents wore (and their parents' parents before them), that made them so different from the Lakefront kids—the richies, preppies, trendies, and school politicians who never set foot in the courtyard.

Andie glanced over at the doorway that led from the school building into the yard. Inside were the worshipers of Izods and buttondowns, blazers and cords, lambswool and linen. Except for changes in size and color, they were already dressed in the uniforms they'd wear for the rest of their lives. Inside were the richies. All of them. Including the incredible disappearing Blane McDonough. Now you see him . . . now you see him!

He was standing in the doorway, looking out over the courtyard. He was watching her. Andie saw him hesitate a moment. His eyes swept the hostile turf between them, taking in the leather jackets and greased-back hair, the boots, braces and Mohawks, the antique clothing and the merely thriftshop. He took a breath, looked over his shoulder to make sure no one was watching him, and eased into the crowd.

Andie almost laughed, seeing him. He'd loosened his tie and opened the top button of his blue buttondown shirt. Now, hands thrust into the pockets of his crisp chinos, he was striding toward her. Nodding politely, smiling nervously, Blane moved through the incredulous Martians of the yard. Andie decided to take pity on him. She gave him a smile.

"How're you doing?" Blane asked gratefully. He sat down next to her on the bench.

"Fine. You?"

"I'm okay," he said. "You?"

She laughed. "I said I was fine."

Blane smiled lamely. "Oh, yeah. Sorry."

"It's okay," Andie said. "This is your first time out here, isn't it?"

"Yeah." He looked around. The freaks were glaring at him. He cleared his throat and turned away from the nasty looks. "I guess I'm not too popular out here."

"You do just fine inside."

"Not really. I'm not all that into it."

"It's okay," Andie said. "I liked your little computer trick."

Blane brightened. "Thanks. I've crashed the entire school district's system."

"You're clever, huh?"

He glanced nervously over his shoulder.

"Are you late for something?" Andie asked.

"Yeah, a little," Blane said, suddenly sounding uncomfortable again. "Look, what I wanted to say was, do you want to go out or something Friday?"

That surprised her. She had to think about it. Being asked out by a cake-eater was something she might have dreamed about—but she'd never actually expected it to hapen. "Friday's okay," she said at last.

"Where do you live?"

Andie's smile faded. She didn't want to tell him.

"Where do you live?" Blane asked again. "I mean, where should I pick you up?"

"At the mall." Andie thought quickly. "Pick me up at Trax."

"Sure."

He got up, planted his hands in his pockets again, and began to back away. "Okay, then," he said. "Right? Okay, I'll see you." Then he turned and headed back across the courtyard, fast.

Steff McKee was waiting for him.

Blane had ducked inside, determined to put as much distance between himself and the freak courtyard as possible. He'd started quickly down the hall when Steff called out to him.

Blane stopped and turned around. "Hey, what's happening?"

"Hey," Steff said, coming up to him. "I was just going to ask you the same thing."

"Nothing too much," Blane said. He was still a little rattled from his trip through the courtyard. "I'm going to class."

Steff smiled slyly. "I saw you outside."

"So?"

"So? What were you doing, Blane?"

"Who are you, my mother?" Blane shot back. He stared at Steff. "I've got to go." He turned and continued down the hall.

Steff followed him. "Seriously, what's going on?"

"Nothing."

"Not nothing, Blane. I saw you rapping all over that zombie."

Blane winced. Zombie? Andie Walsh? What was Steff, kidding? He cocked his head and looked at Steff now—confused and irritated. "So?" he said. "What do you care?"

"My best friend's conversing with a mutant and I'm curious. No reason to flip out."

"Hey, I'm not flipping out. I happen to like her."

"What?" Steff said, acting as shocked as if Blane had gone crazy. "Oh, man," he said, shaking his head sadly. "If you're serious, I'm embarrassed for you."

Blane just looked at him.

Steff was angry now. He wondered just how far things had gone. First there'd been that scene in the record store, and now this. Was Blane, his best friend—his puppet, for Chrissake—going to make out where he'd failed? "You start hanging out with her and you won't have a friend."

Blane bridled. "You included?" he asked coldly.

"You can do a lot better than her, Blane."

It was the wrong thing to say. Steff saw Blane's face go cold. He felt the sudden iciness between them. He'd gone too far. He'd wanted to turn Blane off Andie Walsh—to make him believe that she was nothing, worth nothing. A zoid, a zombie, a big zero. What he definitely did not want was to lose a best friend over a freak like her. He had no intention of cutting Blane loose, of giving him enough slack to stray. No way.

And then it occurred to him: the tighter he held onto Blane the easier it would be for him to get even with Andie Walsh. Cut her down. Put her away, man.

He'd seen her smiling up at Blane out there in the courtyard. Blane could be his hit man. *Bang. You're dead, Andie Walsh.* He'd promised her big trouble. Blane could deliver it—if Steff played it right, if he didn't push him too far, too fast.

Steff smiled now. "Hey, I'm sorry, babes," he said in a lighter tone. "It's your life. It's none of my business."

It took a minute, but Blane let go of it. Deflated, suddenly. The cold anger he'd been building released like a chilly breeze, like air from a snow tire that someone—Steff McKee, for instance—had just punctured.

"You really think she's nothing?" Blane asked.

Steff shook his head, regretfully. "I really do. Sorry." He threw in an affectionate poke on the arm for good measure. Then he resumed his role as Blane's best friend and advisor. "You're late," he said, pointing to the ceiling. Like clockwork. Like always. The bell magically rang, and Steff took off down the hall. He was betting Blane would stare after him for a moment, not knowing what to think.

It was a good bet. Because Steff would have won.

Duckie Dale was in heaven, or the closest thing to it he could imagine. It was dark outside and he was in Andie Walsh's room, sitting on Andie Walsh's bed, with Andie Walsh herself sitting crosslegged not two feet from him.

She had no choice. Every other inch of available space in the room was covered with something. Old clothes were heaped around— jewelry, ribbons, hats, shoes. There were magazines and books everywhere—flaky old magazines, bright shiny new ones, huge faded secondhand books, lavishly illustrated library tomes on fashion, art, and design.

The walls were brimming with posters and fashion illustrations and photographs torn out of magazines and charcoal drawings tacked and taped up between flowing bright scarves and belts and an old kimono and a man's flannel bathrobe with an ancient braided silk rope dangling from its belt loops.

So, basically, there was nowhere else for the two of them to sit except on Andie's bed. And there was nothing separating them but Duckie's homework, which Andie was reading with obvious dismay.

She looked up. "Duckie," she said, "the Warsaw Pact is a treaty signed by the Soviet Union and its seven East European satellites. It established a mutual defense organization as a counterweight to NATO."

Duckie released the pillow he'd been holding. Actually, he'd been cradling it in his arms, stealing an occasional secret sniff of the lingering scent of her cologne. "What'd I put?" he asked.

"You wrote, 'The Warsaw Pact is the pact that's named after Warsaw.'"

"And?"

"A teacher's going to know you're trying to fake it."

"Okay. You're right," Duckie admitted. "What about the rest of it?"

"The Russian Revolution did not take place in Germany."

"What was Karl Marx?" he said. "Was he German or what?"

"He was a German."

"Okay," Duckie said.

"But his being German doesn't have anything to do with where the Russian Revolution occurred."

He stared at her, waiting. She stared at him and shrugged.

"Good point," he said.

Andie set the paper down. "Duckie, can I propose something to you without your getting mad?"

He looked up at the ceiling. "That depends," he said.

"On what?"

He looked at her. "I don't know. I just said that. Sure, go ahead."

"I propose that you're deliberately flunking your classes, Duckie, so that you can stay in high school."

It was as if she'd punched him. He exhaled hard. He reddened, and Andie realized she'd never seen him embarrassed before.

"That's totally absurd," Duckie said fast and defensively. "Why would I do that?"

Her heart ached for him. "I don't know. Tell me."

"I'm not, so there's nothing to tell you."

"You're not always one to face things, Ducks."

"Oh? Since when? What am I not facing?"

"The future," Andie said softly.

He ran his fingers along the seam of her pillow case.

"Whether or not you face the future, it happens. Right?" he said.

"You run yourself down. Why?"

"I'm not running myself down." He shook his head. "Do you think I'm running myself down? I don't think I'm running myself down. Why? Because of my clothes?" he asked her pillow. "No way. Because why? Because I can laugh at myself? That's called a sense of humor. You should get one." He looked up at her at last, and grinned. "They're nice."

Grateful for his grin, Andie reached out and put her hand behind his neck. She pulled him toward her until their foreheads touched. "What are we going to do next year?" she asked, feeling suddenly blue.

"According to you," Duckie said, "I'll still be in high school."

"I'm serious, Duck. Not a day in eight years has passed when I didn't see you or talk to you."

"Devotion, babe," Duckie said sadly.

Andie pulled back and kissed his forehead. "I hope I'm not the only one who knows what an incredible person you are."

"At this point in time, I'm afraid you are."

Andie laughed. She hugged him and felt him shiver suddenly. She stood up with a determined sigh. "Okay. You're getting an A on this paper, Duck. If it takes all night. I'm going to get something to drink, then we work. What do you want?"

"Beer, scotch, Hi-C juice box. Whatever."

She left the room. Duckie stared at the door for a moment. There was a teary feeling in his gut and in his throat. He let out a deep breath, stood up, and wandered through the wonderful mess of Andie's room. At the dresser, he picked up her hairbrush.

"I love this woman," he told the brush. He looked at himself in the mirror. "I love this woman. I have to tell her," he said. "If she laughs, she laughs, but I can't wait anymore."

He saw the torn photograph stuck in the mirror frame. He'd seen it there before, and he knew who the girl in the prom dress was. "If she doesn't love me," he told that girl, "then she doesn't love me. But if I don't find out . . ." Duckie shrugged.

The girl in the prom dress watched him with her mysterious smile. "How could you have left her?" Duckie asked suddenly. "I'd never have. Never." He looked over his shoulder, then turned back to her and continued in a confidential whisper. "But don't worry about it, okay? She's fine. She's going to be all right. I'll take care of her. I love her so bad . . ."

He held the brush up to his mouth like a

microphone and began to hum a 50s tune. Remember that one?" he said to the photograph. "Bet they sang it at your prom, right? Well, this one's for you." Duckie whirled away from the mirror. "And for all you hard-travelin' mothers out there."

He sang into his hairbrush mike and grabbed one of Andie's hats off a wall hook. It was a wide-brimmed man's hat, and it flopped down over his ears. He pushed it to the back of his head and continued dancing through the room until he caught a glimpse of himself in the closet mirror and stopped suddenly.

"She's going to laugh at me," he said. He looked at the hairbrush in his hand. "I can't blame her." He tossed the hairbrush onto her bed and took off the hat.

Duckie walked into the kitchen with his schoolbooks under his arm. Andie had popped a Coke for herself, and she was stabbing a straw into a juice box for him. "I'm going to split," he told her.

"What about your paper?" she asked, surprised.

"That's what I'm going to do." He looked down at his feet. Not that he could've avoided looking at them. They were everywhere. Covered half the kitchen floor, didn't they?

"I'm going to do it myself," he told Andie. "I mean, if you help, it'll be bogus. It won't be my work." He looked up at her. "You're right," he said, "I'm messing up too much." He took the juice box from her. "I'll catch you in the A.M."

Duckie took a sip. "Drinking and driving don't mix. That's why I ride a bike," he said, toasting Andie with the juice.

He opened the kitchen door quickly, and walked into the screen. "Sorry," he said—to whom, the door? Disgusted with himself, he shook his head, opened the screendoor and ran outside to his bicycle. His bicycle! To a rusting, dumb three-speeder that, as far as he could remember, was the best and last present his dad had ever given him. Oh, God, how could anyone respect a guy with only two wheels? He strapped his books to the back of his bike and climbed on. "Crappo!" Duckie hollered, tossing the juice box into the bushes. Then he wheeled the bike around and pedaled away.

Nine

On Friday morning, before gym class, Jena asked Andie whether she was doing anything for the weekend. Andie said, "No. Probably not."

It was weird. She didn't want to tell Jena about her date with Blane. Didn't even want to mention it as a maybe. It wasn't that she was ashamed of going out with a richie. Not exactly. It was just that Jena really hated richies. And Jena had a big mouth sometimes. And, Andie told herself, she just didn't feel like fielding Jena's flack today.

Then how come she felt like such a rat? How come she felt as though having a date with a guy who probably had his jeans dry-cleaned was this absolute criminal act?

They were outside in their gym uniforms sitting with their backs to the wall and smoking. Jena handed Andie the cigarette she had cupped in her palm. "So then what're you going to do? You going to study?" she asked.

Andie took the cigarette and stole a quick puff. "Maybe," she said, handing it back.

Jena hid it behind her back as a couple of

girls walked past. "You study so much it makes me ill," she said. "What's the point?"

"I don't want to work in a record store all my life."

"What're you going to be? A doctor?" Jena said, with a snort of contempt.

The whistle blew. Quickly Jena dropped the cigarette and covered it with her foot as she and Andie scrambled to their feet. Then they joined the rest of the class in front of Mrs. Dietz, the gym teacher.

Benny Trombley was standing next to Jena. Actually, Benny was not standing next to Jena. That was the trouble. She and her friend, Kate Hanson, were making a big thing of leaving plenty of space between themselves and Andie and Jena.

Andie didn't really care. It seemed to her she'd left that kind of caring behind years ago. If she was going to crack up over rejection, it would have been for something that counted, like her mother's taking off. It sure wasn't going to be because a couple of dips got off pretending in gym class that she and Jena smelled bad or something. Andie just sighed, bored again with their baby games. But Jena, as usual, bit the bait. She caught Benny's eye and flipped her the bird.

"Oh, that's classy," Kate Hanson muttered under her breath.

"She really knows how to hurt a girl, doesn't she?" Benny smirked. "Oh, I'm wounded. I don't know if I'll survive."

"You won't if you keep messing with me," Jena growled, a bit too loudly.

Mrs. Dietz blew her whistle. Andie bowed her head. She knew what was coming. Dietz had a history with Jena.

"What was that, Miss Homan?" the gym teacher asked.

"I said, she won't if she keeps messing with me," Jena repeated. She narrowed her eyes at Dietz, daring her to make something of it.

"Won't what?"

"Won't be able to write her phone number on the wall of the boy's john like she usually does, Mrs. Dietz, 'cause I'm going to break her arm."

Kate Hanson cracked up. Benny elbowed her sharply. "Sorry," Kate said.

Mrs. Dietz pointed to the door. Throwing kisses to the gym class, Jena strolled toward it. Andie rubbed her forehead, hiding her eyes, trying not to laugh at Jena—trying not to cry, either, at how dumb Jena was to let them get to her like that.

"Walsh." Mrs. Dietz turned to Andie. "Do you share your partner's attitude?"

She didn't, of course. She thought Jena had a big mouth and a bad temper and that she was a fool to always let those creeps goad her. But Andie couldn't bring herself to say "No." Jena was her friend. Feeling trapped, she looked helplessly at the gym teacher. To her relief, Mrs. Dietz gave her an accepting smile.

Andie glanced at Benny and Kate. Kate

smiled at her and mouthed: "Eat dirt." Benny looked smug and satisfied.

Andie couldn't take it any longer. With weary resignation, she raised her hand. "Mrs. Dietz," she said, "I don't share Jena's attitude, exactly. I think it would be a great loss to the school if they were prevented from writing their names on the wall of the boy's john—"

Jena and Andie sat side by side across the desk from Mr. Donnelly, the principal. Mr. Donnelly looked almost as bored as Jena did, and quite a bit more worn out.

"Jena, I know your problem," he said. "You are just a problem—"

"Thank you, sir." Jena batted her eyelashes at him.

"But," he continued, ignoring her, "I don't understand your problem, Andie."

"Maybe she's sick and tired of being treated like dog dirt," Jena interrupted again.

"I think maybe this discussion would be a little more productive if you were to step outside," Mr. Donnelly told Jena.

"Fine." She stood up. "But that won't change the fact that this school blows."

She strutted out. "I don't know what you see in her, frankly," Mr. Donnelly said to Andie once Jena had gone.

"I don't have to see anything. She's my friend."

"Andie, you've only got a few weeks left. You're doing extremely well in your classes. I think your chances for a scholarship are excellent—"

"I know this, Mr. Donnelly."

"Why now? Why are you in here now?"

"I don't know. I guess I got fed up. Or worn down. Or something."

"With what?"

"With the way we get treated."

"Who's we?" Donnelly asked.

Andie shook her head. "Oh, come on," she said, "you know who."

Mr. Donnelly did understand. He nodded and looked down at his hands, which were folded on the desk. He opened them and folded them again. Then he cleared his throat. "As long as the structure of this community remains as it has for all these years, there are going to be haves and have-nots getting their education side by side."

Andie glared at him. "Don't call me a have-not, Mr. Donnelly," she said coldly. "You can call me a freak or a zoid, but not a have-not."

"I didn't mean . . ."

Andie turned away. She looked at the door. She wanted out.

"You're getting a top-notch education. And I don't want you to throw it away," Mr. Donnelly said quickly. "I don't want you to jeopardize your future with nonsense like this." He stood up abruptly. "All right, you can go now, Andie."

She stood. "What about Jena?" she asked.

"What happens to Jena is no concern . . ."

Mr. Donnelly began. But he glanced at her face and let it go. He looked down at his desk. Then he looked up again—directly at her, this time. "Yes, all right. She can go, too. Tell her it's all right. And, Andie . . . I'm sorry."

It wasn't Jena but Duckie who was waiting for Andie outside Mr. Donnelly's office. "Hey, I heard what happened," he called to her. His feet slapped the hall linoleum as he hurried toward her, coattails flapping. "I came as fast as I could."

Andie groaned. Duckie was always overreacting.

"Was it bad?" he persisted.

"It was nothing, Duckie."

"Are you upset?"

"No."

"Yes you are," he said, his brow furrowed with concern.

Andie sighed and continued down the hall.

Duckie skidded to a stop, made an abrupt turn, and flapped after her. "I know just what to do to make you feel better."

"I feel fine," Andie said wearily.

"I want to take you away this weekend." He smiled brightly at her. "Do you fish?"

She stopped walking and stared at him. Then she said, "I have a class," and turned the corner, leaving him behind.

Duckie gazed after her. "This woman is suffering inside," he murmured.

A jock turned the corner, a football player

or weightlifter—a big guy with shoulders like a Mack truck. The jock looked at Duckie with mild curiosity, then shrugged and elbowed him into a locker.

"Next time, I kill! You hear me?" Duckie shouted at the jock's back. The boy looked over his shoulder at Duckie, who quickly held up one hand like a traffic cop. "Just kidding!" he shouted. The senior turned away again. "Butt-wipe," Duckie grumbled. The boy turned around slowly. Duckie whirled away—right into the cement-hard chest of another All-Star.

They each took an arm and lifted him up between them. Resignedly Duckie threw back his head and raised his feet. They walked him down the corridor like that until they got to the girls' bathroom. Then they recited in unison: "And a one, and a two, and a threeeee!"

Four girls were at the sinks. One was sneaking a smoke. The others were talking and fussing with their hair and makeup as the double doors burst open and Duckie flew in.

The girls screamed.

Duckie picked himself up off the floor and dusted his jacket sleeves. Then he stepped up to the mirror between two of the shriekers. "Hey," he said, checking his hair. "How's it going?"

Ten

One by one the shops in the mall were closing for the night. At Trax, Iona was ringing up the day's sales, or trying to.

"Oh, no. I don't believe it," she groaned, hitting the wrong button on the calculator for the third time.

In pink paisley and thriftshop pearls, Andie was sitting on the counter, looking out the store window, waiting.

"Why can't I do this?" Iona grumbled.

"You have to subtotal first." Andie turned around and slid off the counter to help her. "I tell you that every time."

Iona pinched her cheek gratefully. "One last tune and then it's off to enjoy a horrible relationship," she said, putting on a record as Andie took over the totaling.

Music blasted from the store speakers. Iona laughed. "The furrier next door loves this one."

A sudden frenzied shriek sounded above the music.

Iona and Andie whirled toward the door.

There was Duckie Dale posing dramatically for them outside the store. He paused for a moment. Then, with another wild screech, he launched himself, gyrating and sliding, in front of the window. Crazy, possessed, lip-synching the song, the Duck Man danced, done up in his finest: a huge plaid sportcoat, skin-tight black jeans, workboots, shades, and the old snap-brim hat.

Watching through the window, Andie and Iona exchanged weary looks.

Duckie continued his mad dance outside the store for a moment. Then he stopped just as suddenly as he'd begun. He relaxed. He turned up his coat collar, strolled into the store, and said smoothly, "Good evening, ladies. Good tune."

"We're closed," said Iona.

Duckie leaned toward her across the counter. "You know what an older woman does to me?"

"Changes your diapers?" Iona ventured.

"Touché," said Duckie. "Seriously, you're a very smoky alternative, but—" He pointed to Andie. "This is the Duck Man's love in life." Then, extending his arm to her, he said, "Shall we blast off?"

Andie looked at Iona. "You ever had one of these?" she asked.

Iona looked Duckie over. "I don't think so," she said.

He winked at them. "What do you say, ladies? Let's plow."

It was closing time. Andie headed for the employees' bathroom. Iona went into the back room to turn out the lights. She knocked on the door on her way back to the front of the store. "Andie? Hon, it's after nine," she called. "Don't waste good lip gloss."

Duckie was browsing through a record bin in the thin glow of light from the mall. "You got Ian and Sylvia here?" he asked, not looking up. "Or 'Cherish' by The Association?"

Iona put her arm around his neck. "You are too young to be so old," she said. There wasn't enough light in the store to see whether he'd blushed. She thought he had. She smiled, then went back into the storeroom and tapped lightly at the bathroom door again. "Andie, I don't mean to be a rat, honey," she said softly, "but I don't think Mr. Wonderful's going to happen tonight."

The door opened slowly. "I don't know what I'm doing," Andie said. She'd washed her face and put on new makeup. She looked ravishing, and wretched.

"Wishful making-up," Iona cracked half-heartedly. She put her arm around Andie, who sighed.

Duckie watched them from the storeroom doorway. "You babes are talking sign language that the old Ducker does not understand," he said as he cruised in to join them.

Andie just looked at him and shook her head. Then, arms around each other, she and Iona started out of the back room. Duckie trailed after them, more perplexed than ever.

"Would you people mind helping me out here? I'm confused."

"She got stood up, twerp," Iona said, softly.

"Stood up? How so? I'm here. Is this one of those feminine mystique deals?" he asked.

There was a tap at the front door. Andie looked up and saw Blane McDonough looking in. He was hunched over, peering apprehensively into the darkened record store. She looked at Iona, whose expression of wide-eyed surprise turned quickly into a congratulatory wink.

Duckie turned to see what they were staring at.

Blane rapped on the glass.

Andie waved to him. She and Iona started for the front of the store, leaving Duckie standing a few steps from the storeroom, shocked and confused. It took a minute for him to put it together.

He looked at the guy standing in the doorway. Nothing special: a production-line richie dressed like any other Lake-model richie, in regulation crewneck sweater and wrinkled jacket, khaki pants loose and cool, credit cards smoking up his pockets.

Then Duckie looked at Andie in her thirdhand matching paisley dress and jacket, her pale pink stockings and two-tone thriftshop shoes. She was beautiful. Her shoulders had undrooped. Her swan's neck had uncoiled, her head was high, her face was lit up and happy again.

"Andie?" Duckie said.

He looked from her across the store to the front door and back again—and he had it. "You're kidding," he breathed.

Andie stopped and turned to him. All at once she realized how hurt and confused he was. "Duck, I'm really sorry," she said.

Duckie put his shades back on, fast. "You're going to go out with that guy?"

She took a step toward him. "He's really nice, Duck. You'll like him. He's not like the others."

He backed away from her, shaking his head. "No way, Andie. You really amaze me. They dump all over everybody, including you. I can't believe you're this stupid!"

Iona unlocked the door. She looked Blane up and down carefully. Then she smiled and shook her head. "How come you rich guys are always such handsome hunks?" she said wistfully.

Blane barely heard her. "Huh?" he said. He was watching Andie.

At the back, near the storeroom, Duckie was glaring at her. Andie reached out to him, and he slapped her hand away furiously. "He's going to use you and throw you away," he said. "I would have died for you."

"So what am I supposed to do?" Andie said miserably. "He asked me out. I like him. If I hate him because he's got money, then that's the same thing as people who hate me because I don't."

Duckie just shook his head. "You can't do this and respect yourself," he said. "You just can't."

Andie felt her cheeks becoming hot. "I'll make that decision, okay?" she whispered angrily.

"Sure," Duckie shot back. "You can do what you want."

"You talk like just because I'm going out with Blane—"

"*Blane?*" Duckie snorted. "The guy's name is *Blane?* Get serious!"

"My going out with him," she continued, "doesn't mean we're not friends."

"Oh, is that a fact? Maybe from where you stand. But from where I stand it's a big fat farewell."

Andie took a deep breath. "This doesn't change how I feel about you, Duckie," she said quietly.

"Oh, that's very nice. Here's the point, Andie. I'm not particularly concerned with whether or not you like me." Duckie's voice was breaking with anguish. "I live to like *you*. And I can't like you anymore. So when you get your heart splattered all over hell and you're feeling low and dirty, don't look for this fool to help pump you back up."

"I can't believe you're saying this," she whispered.

"Well, that's just tough." Duckie pushed past her and hurried toward the door. Head down, he slipped past Blane and out into the dark.

In the parking lot, on the way to his car, Blane said, "That guy who was in the store—"

"He's a friend of mine. I've known him since I was a kid." For a second, Andie considered apologizing for Duckie. But she couldn't do that to him—she couldn't be that disloyal. "He's a real nice guy," she said, glancing at Blane. "I like him a lot."

Blane nodded. They walked on, not saying much, stealing looks at one another. Finally, Blane asked, "Do you want to go home and change?"

Andie didn't answer right away. Then she shrugged her shoulders and laughed. "I already did."

"Oh," Blane said. He smiled uncomfortably and nodded. "Yeah, right."

They continued silently through the parking lot.

"Sorry," Blane said.

Andie shrugged again.

After a while, he said, "You up for a party?"

She stopped walking.

"Yes? No?" he asked.

"No," Andie said quietly.

"Why?"

"Why?" She looked up at him.

Blane knew what she meant. "You're with me," he said. "It's okay. These are my friends."

"I *know*," Andie said pointedly.

"I wouldn't take you if I didn't think you'd be okay there. They'll be cool."

"Why don't we go somewhere else?" Andie suggested.

"Listen," Blane said awkwardly. "I like you. I think you like me. We both know there's a lot of garbage that goes on between people around here. But you're above it and I'm above it. And if we're going to make anything happen, we've got to face it."

Andie turned and stared straight into his eyes. Blane fought hard not to turn away. He met her questioning gaze and said, "I have as much to lose as you. We can go do something with your friends. Or we can hide. The choice is yours."

He was right, she knew. She took a deep breath and nodded. Blane put his arm around her. "If it's a bad time," he promised, "we leave."

They were driving through the neighborhood she'd driven through with Duckie. Andie felt a twinge of guilt as she thought of him, and sighed.

"We're almost there," Blane assured her. They turned into a street jammed with carelessly parked cars. At the end of the street, a huge house was ablaze with light. Andie could hear the music all the way from the corner. The eight or nine cars in the big circular driveway in front of the house were even more recklessly

parked than the cars at the curb. The grilles of
Mercedes and Porsches were mashed against
the shrubbery lining the drive, and a little red
Alfa Romeo sat in the center of the manicured
lawn.

It took Andie a moment to realize that this
was her favorite house, the one she'd dreamed
about—the rambling stone mansion with the
white columns and trellised rose gardens.

Her heart pounded. She was grateful for
Blane's arm around her as they walked into the
house. The noise was deafening. She felt nearly
sick with anxiety.

A boy she'd never seen before passed them
as they stood in the foyer. A drunken girl was
clinging to his shoulder. The boy stopped and
offered a sip of his drink to Blane, who refused
it. The girl tried to focus her drunken eyes on
Andie.

Nervously Andie offered her a polite smile.

The girl's eyes widened, and she gasped.
"You're the zoid in my art class!"

Andie turned away.

Blane took her hand and led her out of the
foyer into the living room. The music was even
louder there. The smell of liquor and cigarettes
was almost as powerful as the noise. And there
were kids splayed all over the room. There were
drinks everywhere. Huge plastic Coke contain-
ers lay on their sides, trickling syrupy soda onto
the thick rugs and polished oak floors. Cans of
beer, tumblers of vodka and Scotch left wet
rings on the tables and stuck out from under the

richly upholstered sofas and overstuffed chairs. An athletic supporter had been flung at an oil painting; it dangled from the corner of the elaborate gilt frame. Behind one of the sofas, a girl was clutching a bouquet of peonies and throwing up into the huge ceramic vase from which she'd plucked them.

As Blane led Andie through the living room everyone, except the retching girl, seemed to stop what they were doing to stare at them. Looking straight ahead, Andie followed Blane into the dining room.

A whole table of jocks were sitting there in their underwear, eating TV dinners. They looked blearily up from their food as Blane and Andie walked through. Blane hurried her into the kitchen. Then he turned to her. "I can't believe I actually associate with these people," he said.

"I can't believe I'm actually here," Andie answered, shuddering.

"It's pretty bad, huh?" he said softly.

"Way beyond."

"We'll go upstairs," Blane said.

Andie ripped her hand out of his. "No, thanks."

"What?"

"I didn't come here for that," she said, angrily.

"You think that's what I meant?" Blane laughed nervously. "Hey, I haven't even kissed you yet. Look, it's quieter up there. I swear to God, these hands"—he held out his hands—

"they'll stay in my pockets." He drove his hands into his pockets, then bent over and picked up a stray bag of pretzels with his teeth and snared a six-pack with his elbows. "See?" he said through clenched teeth.

Andie couldn't help smiling.

They went up the back stairs, laughing. The upstairs hall was empty. Blane jerked his head toward a bedroom door. Andie hesitated.

"Give me a break," Blane said. "I'm helpless." He pushed open the door and went inside.

She followed him.

Steff McKee, barechested, was sitting in bed with a sheet pulled up to his waist and a bottle of Scotch in his hand.

He looked up as Blane and Andie walked in. His face froze, then flashed with anger. His nightmare was coming true before his eyes. His best friend and former puppet was succeeding where he had failed. For one split second, Steff glared at Andie with icy hatred. Then he smiled. He even managed a laugh.

"Welcome," he said, toasting them with the Scotch.

Blane and Andie sat down on a loveseat along the wall. "This is Andie," Blane said, setting down the beer. "Andie, Steff."

"It's nice you could come by . . ." Steff cocked his head at her. "It's *Andie*, is it?"

"Yeah," Blane said, innocently. "Andie." He had no idea they knew each other.

Abruptly Steff shifted gears. He clapped his

hands and rubbed his palms together. "Well, so you guys want the bed?" he asked graciously.

"No, we're fine," Blane said, casting a nervous glance at Andie.

"This is the last serious high school party of my career," Steff announced. "I hope you guys can tough it out until Sunday night when the folks return home. This one might kill the old man."

Blane chuckled. Andie glanced out the window behind her. So this was Steff's house. She might have known.

The bathroom door opened. Andie saw the light reflected in the dark window and turned. Benny Trombley staggered out of the bathroom. She was barefoot and wearing a raincoat.

"One small step for Benny; another giant step for mankind," she said, flinging open the coat to reveal her bikini underwear.

Andie looked away in disgust. Steff toasted Benny. "Is she a tramp or what?" he said.

Benny staggered over to the bed and sat down. Then she looked over at Blane and Andie. "Oh, my God! Am I having a nightmare? I know you!" she shrieked.

Andie faked a smile.

"You're in my calculus class."

"Gym," Andie reminded her.

"Your name is Jim?"

Steff laughed. "Is this girl worthless?" he said, shaking his head at Benny.

Suddenly Benny reared up drunkenly.

"You and your friend made fun of me in gym!" she growled.

"Benny," Blane said, "why don't you take it easy?"

"This is Steff's party, Blane. Don't tell me what to do."

"Steff?" Blane said.

"You shouldn't be allowed to just bring anybody you want!" Benny shouted at Blane.

Steff bunched the sheets around himself and slid out of bed. He took Benny's hand.

"She's going to ruin my night," Benny protested.

"Shut up, Benny," Blane said.

"You're a jerk, Blane."

Steff tugged at Benny's hand. "Come on. I think Blane needs the room, Ben," he said. He smiled at Andie. "Isn't she a pain?" he asked, and led Benny to the door. She turned back to Blane and Andie.

"You're a complete moron, Blane," she said. "And you!" she shrieked at Andie. "I don't even know what you are."

"You guys have a good time," Steff said, pushing Benny out the door. He looked at Andie with a sly smile, then turned to Blane. "Let me know how she is," he said. He laughed and closed the door.

Andie was fighting back tears of rage.

Blane said softly, "They're jerks when they drink." She glared at him. *Jerks?*

"I'm sorry," Blane said. "It was a rotten idea."

He leaned over and tried to kiss her.

Andie moved her head away. "Get me out of here."

"We're alone now," he protested.

"I said, get me out!"

Blane took her arm. "I won't take you home."

Andie's eyes were blazing.

"I want to be with you," Blane explained. "If not here, then somewhere else."

She held her stare.

"I'm sorry. I overestimated my friends. I made a mistake. An *honest* mistake. You want to hit me?"

"Yes," Andie said without hesitation.

Blane shut his eyes and pointed to his chin. "Fine," he said, and then he smiled.

Eleven

Duckie was inside Cats at last.

"I can't believe it," he said to Iona. The place was hot, dark, and humid with sweat. The music was thundering. They were in the quietest corner they could find, hunched over a table. They'd been sharing the table, and a couple of pitchers of beer, for about an hour.

Beer was not Duckie's drink. Orange juice, Hi-C, the occasional Kool Aid, he could handle. So right now he wasn't sure whether it was the beer or Iona speaking, but someone was telling him a tragic story of true love.

"The bum tied me up." Iona shook her head sorrowfully. "That's his thing."

"No," said Duckie sympathetically. "You want to know my thing? If I really have it solid for a girl, you know? I ride by her house on my bike. Man, I'll do it like a hundred times in a single day."

"You ever park?"

"Nope. I'm a full-on drive-by guy," Duckie said, looking into the bottom of his glass. He could still see the reflection of the whirling overhead lights in the glass. That's how he knew there was some beer left. He downed it.

Iona sighed. "I guess I'd rather have a dude riding his bike past my house than tying me to the bathroom sink."

Duckie lowered his shades seductively. "Give me your address," he said. Then, over his lowered shades, he suddenly saw Andie pushing through the jam of people near the door. The richie was trailing her. For a minute Duckie looked as though someone had kicked him in the stomach. Struggling to regain his composure, he elbowed Iona and pointed them out. "Someday," he confided, "that girl's going to realize what she missed."

"I hope not," Iona said.

The music ended. Duckie dropped his glasses and whistled and stomped. "More!" he shouted. "Gimme more! Yeah!"

Andie recognized his voice. She looked around and saw them. Her face lit up with happy surprise, and she started toward their table.

Duckie turned away, but Iona stood up and waved her over. Andie pushed through the crowd and sat down with them. She kissed Iona.

"Prince Charming wimp out?" Iona asked, looking over Andie's shoulder for Blane.

"He's at the bar. Duck?" Andie said.

Duckie refused to acknowledge her.

"He's sulking," Andie explained to Iona.

"He's not riding his bike past your house anymore either," Iona said.

"Duckie, you're being a real jerk!" Andie snapped.

He turned to her, raised his shades, stared blankly at her for a minute; then dropped the shades and turned away again.

"How'd he get in here?"

"I said he was my kid," Iona told her.

"How come you're here?"

"That—" Iona sighed heavily. "I have been trying to figure that out all night."

Andie looked up in time to see Blane working his way through the throng with a couple of drinks. He looked about as comfortable among the freaks at Cats as she'd felt among the richies at Steff's bash. As he neared the table, a towering, creepily thin guy in a sack dress stopped him and felt his tweed sportcoat lapel. Blane smiled up at the guy. "Gross, isn't it?" he said. The guy released his lapel. "Yeah, well," Blane said, "enjoy your evening."

He scanned the tables. "This is the worst place I've ever been in my entire life," he muttered, craning his neck as he looked for Andie.

He saw her waving to him, and hurried to the table. The closer he came, the lower Duckie sank in his seat. Blane set down the drinks and joined them.

"You met Iona, right?" Andie said.

"Not formally. Hi." Blane offered his hand

to Iona. She shook it, flashing Andie an "I'm-impressed" look out of the corner of her eye.

"And that's Duckie Dale behind the glasses."

"Hi, Duckie," Blane said.

Duckie lifted his glasses. "Philip F. Dale to you, scumwad," he said. Then he groaned and lowered his glasses.

"Er, where've you guys been?" Iona said, trying to cover for Duckie.

"A friend was having a party," Blane said. Then he looked over at Andie, and they laughed together.

Duckie groaned again. "How adorable!"

Andie scowled at him. Blane continued, to Iona, "It was a little . . . intense."

"*You* had an *intense* party?" Duckie said sarcastically.

Blane didn't even notice the insult. "I said it was a friend's party," he explained earnestly.

"Shut up, Duckie," Andie warned.

"What's the problem?" Blane asked her.

Duckie chuckled derisively. He poked Iona. "Classic piece of work there," he said.

"Duckie, please—" Andie urged.

"*Phil.*" He cut her off.

Blane turned to Duckie. "I think you're making Andie uncomfortable. Why don't you knock it off?" he said.

Duckie lifted his glasses again. Then he clutched his stomach, bobbed his head, and pantomimed a phony laugh. Pointing to Blane, he looked at Iona. "I devoted my entire life to the girl. This guy walks in and in one day thinks he knows her. *That's* funny." To Blane, he said, "You should give David Letterman a ring sometime. He'd book you in a minute."

"*Phil*," Andie growled. "Do you want us to leave?"

Duckie winced. "Very perceptive," he snapped.

Andie picked up her drink. Blane stood quickly to hold her chair for her. Duckie laughed.

"The manners on this guy! Andie, this was indeed a treat. Thanks a million," he said grandly.

She scowled at him. "I can't believe I actually felt bad for you tonight," she said. Then she turned her back on him. "See you," she said to Iona, and dashed off into the crowd.

"Nice meeting you, Iona," Blane said.

She waved. "Yeah. Sorry."

"No problem."

"*Noooo* problem," Duckie mimicked him.

"You're a real jerk," Blane said.

"Coming from you, I take that as a compliment."

Blane walked away. Duckie watched him with a bitter, hate-filled stare. Iona put her arm around Duckie. "It's okay, Ducks," she crooned.

Duckie ignored her. "Andie! Yo!" he bellowed.

Andie turned back to the table.

Duckie grabbed Iona and kissed her passionately on the lips. Iona was too stunned to move.

Mopping his brow, Duckie scrambled to his feet. His carefully arranged wave was reared straight up. His lips were smeared with Iona's bright red lipstick. His glasses were askew and blazing with disco lights. He looked like a deranged clown.

"*Noooo* problem, Andie!" he hollered. "You've been replaced!" He waited until she was out of sight. Then he sank back down into his seat, put his head in his hands, and groaned miserably.

Blane and Andie walked out into the cool night air. "I shouldn't have said that to him," Blane said. "It was stupid of me to lose it like that."

Andie took his arm. She was about to answer when a voice called out, "Andie!"

Andie looked across the street. Jena and Simon were climbing out of his car. Jena waited for a passing car, then hurried across the street. Simon followed leisurely at his usual iron-poor pace.

Andie glanced up at Blane and then back at Jena hurrying toward them. "Oh, God," she murmured.

"What?" Blane asked.

Jena's step lost its bounce as she spotted Blane with Andie. She stepped up onto the curb with Simon a few feet behind her. Andie drew a deep breath. Holding Blane's arm, she led him over to them. Blane had his hands in the pockets of his khakis. He looked bright, open, friendly—a perfect prep.

"Hi, Jena—Simon," Andie said apprehensively.

Jena narrowed her eyes at Blane. "This is Blane," Andie said quickly. She was smiling too brightly, talking too fast. "Blane, this is Jena, and that's Simon."

Blane offered his hand. No one reached for it. He withdrew it slowly and tried to maintain his good-natured grin in the frigid silence.

"Weelll, how very interesting," Jena drawled.

"I don't need any crap," Andie said.

"Oh, yeah?" Jena put her hands on her hips and cocked her head at Blane. She looked him up and down. "It looks like you already got plenty. Come on, Simon." She flounced past them toward the club.

"Thanks, Jena," Andie murmured. "Thanks a lot." Jena ignored her.

Andie turned to Blane. "I guess it's my turn to be sorry," she said.

"We're about even, I guess."

She offered him a weak smile, and they started across the street together.

"Now what?" Blane asked.

"I have to work tomorrow. Maybe we should just kiss it off."

"Home?"

Andie stiffened suddenly, trapped. She hadn't wanted him to pick her up at home, but she'd never thought about the return trip. Now, thinking about the squat, ugly bungalow she lived in—comparing it to Steff's place, and what Blane's house must look like, and Benny's, and the girls Blane was used to dating—made her suddenly shudder with shame.

"What?"

"I don't know," Andie said miserably.

"You want to go to my house?" Blane offered.

"I can't."

They reached his car. He opened the door for her. "Do you want to get something to eat, then?"

"No," she said, "I don't . . ."

"Andie, what's wrong?"

She waited outside the car. "I don't want to go home, okay?"

"What's the matter?"

"Nothing," she insisted.

"Something's the matter." He was smiling at her. She looked down the dark street. "Tell me, please," Blane said.

Andie wiped away a tear.

"What did I do?" he asked, concerned.

She shook her head.

"Come on, Andie. What?"

She looked up at him. "I don't want to go home."

"Are you in trouble?"

"No!"

"Then what?!"

"I don't want you to take me home, okay?"

She paused. "I'm not real happy about where I live. All right?"

"Why?"

"Why?" she echoed, staring at him as if the answer should have been obvious.

"Oh," Blane said, finally. Then, "I don't care where you live."

"I do," she shot back. She wiped her eyes on her sleeve and tried to compose herself. "Let's just go, okay? I feel like a fool."

"Andie," Blane began, "I don't care about . . ."

She got into the car. "Go!" she ordered.

The house was dark. Blane parked out front. Andie's eyes were red from crying. Sullen and silent, she stared straight ahead, beyond the railroad trestle at the end of the street to the factory smokestacks silhouetted against the moonlit sky. As uncomfortable as she, Blane followed her gaze. He didn't look at her house.

"I'm sorry about bumming out the night for you," she said.

"You didn't bum out anything. I had a great time," he said unconvincingly.

"Liar."

"I had a good time. I was with you. If I were in a Turkish prison with you, I'd have a good time."

She glanced gratefully at him. Then her eyes brimmed again. "This is just all too weird for me, I guess. It shouldn't happen. It's just too stupid."

"You and me?"

She slid down in the seat.

"Maybe it's—maybe it doesn't happen all the time," he argued gently, "but that doesn't make it wrong. It doesn't mean we can't try."

Andie looked over at him. He smiled at her. She tried to smile back. Her lips were quavering. Her brown eyes were shining with tears, and teardrops trembled on her long dark lashes.

"Andie, what if—?" he said, softly. "Listen, would you feel any better if I asked you to the Prom?"

Andie turned slowly toward him. Her mouth dropped open. A teardrop brimmed over her lid and coursed down her cheek. Blane reached over and caught it on his thumb. "I know the Prom's pretty lame, and I could see why you wouldn't—" he began.

Andie searched his eyes, and he stopped speaking. She touched his lips gently. Then she leaned forward and kissed him.

Blane put his arms around her and pulled her close to him. She framed his face with her palms and, gently holding his cheeks, she kissed him again. This time it was not a kiss of gratitude, but of love. All her feelings—the fear, confusion, and misery of the night, the desire and excitement, the incredible courage she'd called forth in herself and the courage and love she saw now in him—all her feelings went into that kiss.

She pulled back and looked at his face again. Her gaze was strong and serious.

Blane met it. He held her gaze until he knew exactly whom he had kissed. He saw her pride and confidence in herself, her certainty of who she was and what she wanted. He held her look as long as he could, and when he finally looked away, he felt changed forever. He felt as though Andie Walsh's kiss had drained all the boy out of him and turned him into a man.

Twelve

Andie's father was in his room, reading and smoking a cigarette. Andie was surprised to see him in so early. "Hi!" she said. "Guess what?"

He looked up. He could see from the proud and happy look on her face that something wonderful had happened.

"What?" he asked, sitting up abruptly and putting out his cigarette.

"He asked me."

Jack cracked a smile. "And?"

"I accepted." She walked over to the chair beside his bed, took the ashtray off it, and sat facing him on the edge of the seat.

"Congratulations," her father said. "Is this going to mean a little less moping around the house waiting for the phone to ring?"

Andie smiled.

"You in love?" Jack asked.

"Don't embarrass me."

"I'm asking a legitimate question," he protested. "I'm not asking you to go to church in a bathrobe, I'm just asking if you're in love."

110

She tilted her head and thought about it. "Yes," she said.

"You look well kissed." He grinned.

She gave him an affectionate shove.

"I'm just making an honest observation," Jack said.

"I'm not *well* kissed. One kiss." She looked at him, then looked away. "He's a richie," she said.

"A whatie?"

"His family has a lot of money."

"So? Is that a problem?"

Andie shrugged and looked away again.

"Is that why you didn't bring him in?" Jack asked.

"No," she said defensively. "No. He had to get home. He'll come over another time. I'm just not sure about anything. His friends all have money. He has money. I'm not sure they'll accept me."

"Why wouldn't they? You're not putting out an attitude, are you?"

"Not really," she said, thinking about it. "It's just that his doesn't happen very often. People at school stay pretty much to their own kind."

"What's that mean? You like him. He likes you. What his friends say shouldn't mean anything."

"It's my friends, too." Andie shrugged. "It's just everything. I'm not sure about it."

"You take a little heat. It's worth it if you care about him."

"Is it?"

"In my book," her father said soberly.

"Am I overreacting?"

"Hey." He smiled again. "A good kiss can scramble anybody's thoughts. Don't worry about it."

Andie sighed. "Thanks," she said. She leaned over and gave him a hug. Then she stood up.

"You know the only thing that beats falling in love?" Jack said.

"Sure," she said. "A royal flush. Right?" He nodded, and she smiled at him. "Good night."

"Kid?" he called as she started out the door.

She stopped and turned to him.

"I didn't mean to embarrass you."

"I know."

"I'm sorry I'm the one you have to talk about these things with."

Andie flinched. "Don't," she said sharply. Then she eased up and smiled at him again. "I'm not sorry," she said. "She couldn't have said it any better than you."

"I want to know all the gory details!" Iona closed her kitchen window to shut out the shrill sounds of Chinatown on Saturday morning.

Iona lived above Hong's Laundry and the Golden Dragon bakery. Her apartment was always filled with delectable scents: the crispy-clean smell of Clorox, starch, and ironing; the sweet, hot breath of doughy steamed buns.

If the hustle and bustle, the scents and street noises were of another world, the furnishings were of another time. Blond wood and yellow Formica, kidney-shaped tables with wrought-iron legs, zebra-skin seat covers, green parchment lampshades, and decals of pink seahorses with bubbly breath—a Fifties time capsule seemed to have exploded all over her apartment.

And in her hair. This morning, Iona was sporting a foot-high lacquered beehive.

"Everything!" she insisted, carrying the coffee tray from the kitchen to her bedroom—a fluffy shrine of Fifties girlhood—where Andie waited. "I mean, the mingling breath and heaving chests, glowing hearts, pounding passions . . ."

Andie was looking through the open closet at Iona's wardrobe. "I hate to disappoint you," she said as Iona set the tray down on the ruffled rosebud bedspread and rubbed her hands together expectantly. "Nothing happened."

"Nothing?"

Andie looked over her shoulder. Iona was pouring coffee into little plastic cups. Andie shook her head. "I kissed him."

"Strong lips?"

"How do you tell?"

"Did you feel it in your knees?" Iona asked.

"Strong lips," Andie said.

"You know, your little Duckling's got a mean case of the blues."

Andie thought about Duckie and sighed. "I know," she said. A moment ago she'd felt happy and warm, all wrapped up in love. Now, the thought of the Duck Man out in the world alone sent a remorseful chill through her.

Iona sat cross-legged on the bed and took a sip of her coffee. "He said he was going to meditate you out of his memory."

Andie forced a smile and turned back to the closet. "He could probably do it, too." Something caught her eye. She separated it from the other clothes. In a plastic drycleaning bag was a carefully preserved old formal. Andie took it out of the closet.

Iona walked to her vanity and checked herself out in the mirror.

"You want to talk about lips," she said. "I'm old enough to be his mother. And when he threw that kiss on me last night, my flanks went up in flames. I swear. He must practice on melons or something."

Andie took the dress off the rod and turned from the closet with it. "Is this your prom dress?"

Iona turned, saw the dress, and smiled. "Believe it or not," she said, nodding. "Haven't seen it in a while."

"It's great."

"Of course, you'd think so. It's pink." Iona took the dress from Andie and peeled off the plastic.

"I'm going, you know," Andie said. "To the Prom. That sounds so weird. He asked me."

Iona was studying the dress. "Hang on a minute," she said, excited suddenly. "You just wait there." She grabbed the dress and rushed out of the room with it.

A little while later, as Andie was finishing her cup of coffee, the stereo came on with a blast. "Cherish"—the sugary Association ballad—filled the apartment. And Iona's hand, in a long white glove, appeared in the bedroom doorway, beckoning Andie to the living room.

Dressed in the beautiful pink prom dress, her makeup light and girlish, her hair out of its crusty beehive, brushed and shining, Iona whirled for Andie and then began to dance with a phantom partner.

Smiling, Andie watched. Iona looked youthful and happy, and very vulnerable, she thought. It was as if another self had been trapped in the folds of the dress—a softer, happier Iona who had been hidden in the closet, wrapped in tissue paper and preserved in plastic, all these years.

The song ended. "I love this dress," Iona said. "It's beautiful."

"It is," Andie said softly. "I'm sorry, but I've got to go. I'm opening the store today."

"Right," Iona said, smoothing the skirt of the pink formal. "My mother bought it for me. She was so happy. It was the first and last time I looked normal. It would have been a fairy tale if my date hadn't been the only one at the prom with a wife and two kids."

She hurried to the phonograph to remove the record. "You want to try it on? It'll probably fit you better. Your butt is fifteen years younger than mine. Boy, I used to love my butt. It was such a great butt. I wish I had photographs."

"Iona, you're going to OD on nostalgia." Andie laughed.

"Probably. I loved 'The Big Chill.' You want to try it on?"

"Not right now," Andie said reluctantly.

"That's right. You've got to open. I have to get ready myself."

"You're not coming in today, are you?"

"Nope," Iona said. "I'm going out. New guy. Terrance something or other. He owns a pet-store. We'll see what happens." She gave Andie a peck on the cheek. "Go, go. And give Mr. Perfecto a squeeze for me."

Andie smiled shyly.

"And if you see your little Duck Man, be kind, baby. He's nursing some fairly serious wounds."

The living room was filled with flowers. Jack scratched his head as the delivery man set down the last arrangement.

"Are these for your wife?" the man asked.

"No. My daughter, I guess."

"Is she an opera singer or something?"

"Not that I'm aware of," Jack said.

"Well, that's the last one." Jack held the door open for the delivery man, then turned to survey the living room again. He shook his head with wonder. Then he plucked an envelope off one of the arrangements and opened it up.

The card read: "Blane loves Andie!"

Thirteen

At Steff McKee's house, the party was still going on. The front lawn was awash with beer cans and booze bottles. Five or six cars were still parked outside, including the little red Alfa, which had been rolled over onto its side.

The quietest place in the house had turned out to be the library, which was a splendid walnut-paneled room with a massive desk and a leather couch. Steff was rolling joints at the desk.

"That was very uncool of you last night," he said to Blane, who was sitting across the room on the couch.

There was no way Blane could have avoided being Steff McKee's best friend. Their folks saw each other socially. Their fathers had prepped together in the dim and distant past. The boys had gone to the same schools since kindergarten and, as infants, had even shared a governess for two weeks one summer when Steff's nanny quit without giving notice. For as long as Blane could remember, Steff—who was naturally outgoing, competitive, and adventuresome, had been the leader, and Blane—basically easygoing and even-tempered—had been content to be "Steff McKee's best friend."

So, instead of arguing now, which wasn't his thing anyway, Blane played dumb. "What was uncool?"

Steff wasn't buying it. "You know what. I wasn't *that* drunk."

"You mean Andie?" Blane said evenly.

"Yeah." Steff ran his tongue across the rolling paper and twirled the joint between his fingers. "I mean Andie."

"What's the big deal? I like her. As a matter of fact, I'm a little ticked off at all of you guys for being so rude to her."

"It was way out of order for you to foist her on the party."

Blane shook his head. "Can you hear yourself, Steff? Do you hear the same dumb garbage I'm hearing?"

Steff put the joint down with the others he'd rolled. "Do I have to spell it out for you?"

"I guess so."

"Nobody appreciates your sense of humor. In fact, everybody's just about to puke from you. If you're hot for trash, don't show it around us, pal."

"*Buddy,*" Blane corrected.

"I don't need a lot of crap on this one, Blane. I really don't."

Blane fought the urge to leap forward and punch Steff in the teeth. Instead he leaned back on the couch and kept his hands palms-down

119

on the leather. He fought the lump rising in his throat. He couldn't believe Steff was doing this to him. "Is money all that matters to you?" he asked, just managing to hang onto his cool.

Steff snorted contemptuously. "Would I treat my parents' house like this if money was any kind of issue?" He swept the joints into his hand and dumped them into his shirt pocket. "Why are you doing this? Why don't you just nail her and get it over with? Why are you getting involved?"

"Is there something wrong with that? Is there something *inherently* wrong with it?"

"It's just stupid," Steff said. "It's pointless. You're making a fool of yourself. I mean, in a month we're going to be in Chile skiing into the best tans of our lives and you want to ruin it. Why?"

Blane looked away.

"I haven't even mentioned your parents," Steff added. "Won't they be thrilled?"

"They don't have anything to do with this," Blane said softly.

Steff laughed. "Oh, really? I've seen your mother work on you. It's vicious. When Bill and Joyce get through with you, you'll be dogmeat, Blane-babe."

Blane stared up at him. Score one for Steff. His parents probably would chew him up if they found out. They practically had him engaged to Kate Hanson. And they were bound to find out, especially since Steff wasn't going to help him keep Andie a secret.

"I'm getting bored with this conversation."
Steff stood up. "You want her? Take her. But if
you do, that's it. You won't have a friend. Me
included."

"Is that right?" Blane said evenly.

Steff's temper ignited. "Yeah, that's right!"
He came around the desk. "You want to make
the choice? Make it. If that's what friends mean
to you, do it!" He took a breath and downshifted
suddenly. "I personally wouldn't trash a friendship," he said, with a show of containing
himself. "But I'm old-fashioned."

"Steff?" Blane said quietly. "A friend would
understand."

"That's great. Go write a poem." He walked
to the door, then stopped with his hand on the
knob and turned around. "I'm being real nice
about this, Blane. It could get a lot worse. Trust
me," Steff said, and walked out.

"Trust me."

"You're kidding," Andie had replied, as
Blane drove through the main gates of the Hunt
Club.

Up on the hill, the clubhouse—a three-
story plantation-style mansion—had been
ablaze with light. Dance music flowed faintly
through the open windows, and the sounds of
glasses clinking, murmured conversation, and
an occasional laugh broke the night's gentle
stillness.

"Aren't you?" she'd asked, sliding low in
the front seat and pulling her silk neck scarf up

over her nose so that she'd wound up looking like a bandit. "This is the 'special, secret place' you told me about?"

"Trust me," Blane had repeated, looking over at her and laughing.

She had. And he had skirted the clubhouse and driven out beyond it along a darkened road lined with poplars, toward a huge corral. The trees seemed to have walled off the saccharin dance music. In the country darkness, the only noises she'd heard were crickets chirping, the whinnying of a horse, and the rustling of leaves caught in a mild rush of night wind.

Now here they were, inside a very posh horse house, dark except for the outdoor security floodlights that flowed through the shutters and sent slivers of light through the stable walls. Now here they were, sitting together on sweet-smelling bales of soft, prickly hay. Here they were holding hands and staring up at the high beamed stable roof and smiling at nothing.

"Two weeks ago, if somebody had said I'd be going out with a richie . . ." Andie mused.

"A what?"

She laughed. "A richie. I never would have believed it."

"What about me and a zoid?" Blane said, turning to look at her.

"A what?"

He grinned. "You know what? You're not so bad."

"Thank you."

"You know what I mean."

"I know what you mean," she admitted, putting her forehead against his. "It's so insane that someone you don't know, never met, never talked to can be your enemy."

"We haven't even gotten to parents yet," he said.

Andie sat up and hugged her knees. "There's no problem on my end. I've only got one, and he's cool."

"You don't want to know mine," Blane said.

"Okay."

"I think they still believe in arranged marriages—corporate families replacing royal families. I'm the crown prince of McDonough Electric."

She laughed and kissed his cheek. "Irrelevant."

"No."

"Yes." She kissed his lips. "Yes," she said again.

"I just tell them to buzz off?" Blane said.

"Tell them to buzz off," she said.

"Friends, parents . . ."

"Everybody."

"What about you?"

"It's simple," she said, looking at him seriously but unable to contain her smile. "If people don't believe in me, I can't believe in them." She kissed him again.

He took her shoulders and pulled her back gently. "You're not lying, are you?"

"I don't have to lie." She kissed the tip of

his nose. "I live on the outside. There's something to be said for having nothing—"

He drew her close. "Nothing's going to change my mind, Andie," he whispered in her ear. "This is going to happen. Nothing stops it." And then he put his arms around her and kissed her, and for a while, everything they had to say to each other was said without words.

Fourteen

Andie squared her shoulders, straighted her skirt, and strolled across the mall to Magique. The automatic double doors slid back. Andie took a deep breath and stepped into the plush carpeting and perfumed elegance of the mall's poshest clothing store.

The music might have been piped in from the Hunt Club, along with the pair of fashionable matrons sitting in front of the dressing rooms—one on a white brocade Victorian settee, the other overflowing a spindly-legged gilt chair.

For a moment or two, Andie browsed among the dresses undisturbed. Then she drew out a handsomely-cut floor-length gown and examined it at arms' length.

Immediately a tailored salesgirl was at her side. "Can I help you?" the girl asked with a smile.

Andie stiffened and shook her head.

"Something for the Prom?" the salesgirl asked.

She shook her head again, too nervous to speak.

"Well, if you need anything . . ." the girl said, letting it trail.

Andie smiled. The salesgirl backed away, looking her over from head to toe. Then she shook her head, puzzled, and moved on to another customer.

Andie waited until the girl was gone before she lifted the gown's price tag.

Six hundred and fifty dollars.

She gulped, and then looked quickly over her shoulder to make sure the salesgirl hadn't heard her.

But the salesgirl was fawning over the lady on the Victorian settee. At the woman's request, she scurried over to one of the dressing-room doors and tapped lightly at it. The door opened—and Benny Trombley swirled out in a strapless, ice-blue satin gown.

Instinctively Andie stepped back out of sight. She could see Benny and then, as the other dressing room door opened, Kate Hanson, in a flowing ruffled gown. The girls walked over to the seated women. Rolling their eyes with disgust, they modeled the dresses for their mothers.

Andie could see Benny's mother nodding and smiling her approval.

"It stinks," Benny said.

"It's very becoming," her mother insisted.

"Oh, please, Mother." Benny walked over to the rack where Andie had been browsing.

Andie saw her coming and turned to leave.

The automatic doors behind her opened and Chessy Edwards, one of the richies who'd laughed at Jena in English class, waltzed in with her mother. Andie was trapped.

Benny walked to the rack. Without even glancing at the price tag, she yanked off the dress Andie had looked at.

Andie pressed herself against the wall.

But Benny spotted her out of the corner of her eye. She turned and looked Andie up and down. Her mouth fell open in exaggerated shock. Then she narrowed her eyes and said, "The Prom? *You?*"

Andie met her gaze without expression.

Benny shook her head. "You've got to be kidding. Really," she said.

At last Andie moved. She pushed off the wall and hurried past Benny toward the door. Her purse caught on a display of shoes and knocked it over. Andie whirled around, trying to keep the display from crashing down, but she only succeeded in scattering the shoes. With an embarrassed smile to the stunned salesgirl, she threw up her arms and bolted from the store.

At the other end of town, three miles west of the mall, Jack sat on a folding chair outside a curtained dressing room, waiting for the Best-4-Less saleslady to show him the gown he'd asked her to model.

Best-4-Less had no carpeting, no music, and no perfume, except for the gallon jugs of

127

Best-4-Less Bath Splash piled in a pyramid near the marked-down quilted floral bedspreads and chenille rugs with portraits of the Presidents on them.

"I've never had anyone buy a prom dress as a surprise," the saleslady called to Jack from behind the curtains.

Toying nervously with his hat, Jack looked over his shoulder at the mothers and daughters picking out clothes from huge, jumbled bins.

"I've also never modeled a dress before," the saleslady continued. "But if you think your daughter's my size, then we should be in good shape."

Jack nodded even though she couldn't see him. Then he realized it, and felt like a fool. "She loves pink," he called.

"What young lady doesn't?"

Jack shrugged. Then shook his head. He'd done it again.

The saleslady never noticed. "This is a lovely item," she continued. "I like it very much. It's got a real young feel. Ready?"

He straightened up. The dressing-room curtain swept back, and the middle-aged saleslady stepped out wearing a pink floor-length formal. Jack tilted his head this way and that. He thought maybe the gown looked a little out of date on the overweight saleslady. And he wondered if it wasn't too fussy, what with the make-believe roses and pleated bust and the low-slung look of the waistline. Also, it didn't exactly flow the way he'd thought it might when he'd pulled it off the table full of sale gowns.

"And an absolute steal at $49.95," said the saleslady, twirling for him.

By the time Andie got home, the embarrassment and shame she'd felt about practically wrecking Magique had subsided, and she began to see the humor in the situation. And she wanted to share it with Blane.

She wanted to tell him what a jerk she'd been, trying to hide from Benny and then trying to split quietly and taking down half the elegant store on her way out. She was sure he'd understand and laugh about it with her.

He didn't usually laugh all that much. Mostly he smiled. She'd been looking forward to making him laugh.

She checked her phone messages and was a little surprised that he hadn't called her since then. Well, he'd probably been busy. Before she made too much of it, she decided to phone him. She found his phone number in the school directory and called his house.

His mother or his maid—at first Andie wasn't sure which—said, "Who?" and made her repeat her name three times. It turned out to be his mother. She said, "He's probably still at Steff McKee's house. Do you have their number?"

Andie said, "Just tell him that I called. Ask him to call me, please."

Blane's mother said, "Andie Welch, you said? Do we know you?"

"Andie *Walsh.* I go to school with Blane."

"Oh? That's odd. He's never mentioned an Andie. Do I know your mother?"

"I don't think so," Andie said. "Just ask him to call me, please."

"Walsh?" Mrs. McDonough said. "Not Prescott Walsh's daughter?"

"No. I'm sorry."

"Of course. What am I thinking of? Prescott hasn't got a daughter."

While she waited for Blane to call back, she thought she'd let Iona know what she'd done at the mall. But Iona was out with Terrance, or at least that was the message she'd left on her answering machine for Tyrone. Actually, the message was, "Tyrone, don't bother calling again. I'm all tied up." And then there was a maniacal giggle. "With Terrance," Iona said. "And this time it's love, not handcuffs. Everyone else, leave a message."

Andie smiled. She hung up and began to dial Duckie's number. Then she remembered. She wasn't Duckie's friend anymore. She considered hanging up before the phone rang, but there wasn't time.

It didn't matter anyway. Duckie wasn't home either. "I think he's moved in with his brother again," his mother said airily. "But I'm not sure.

Andie dialed Duckie's brother's house. No one there had seen him for a couple of days.

She waited half an hour, then phoned

Blane again. This time a man answered the phone. He said he'd give Blane her message.

Jena was out with Simon.

She called Simon's house. Simon's father said, "Simon who? He don't live here. He stops by to clean out the refrigerator, grub money, and change his boots." Then he hung up on her.

It was nearly dark outside the last time she tried phoning Blane, clutching the receiver so hard her knuckles went white. But he still wasn't there. At least it was the maid who answered this time. "If he calls or comes home, will you tell him to call Andie Walsh?" she said. "He'll know who it is."

She hung up, lay back on the bed, and stared at the ceiling. "Where is he?" she murmured, and then she turned up her blaster and patted the bed for Ace to jump up and join her. He did, immediately. And she hugged him, and sighed.

Ace stirred, whimpering in his sleep. Andie sat up. She must have dozed off; it was dark outside. She heard her father's car wheezing and squeaking into the driveway. Before he came in, she quickly checked her message machine. She hadn't missed any calls.

"Don't fall in love, Ace," Andie whispered. "It's very complicated. You won't like it."

"Andie? You home?" her father yelled.

"In my room," she called. Ace groaned and jumped off the bed as Jack knocked on the door.

"Come in," Andie called.

He looked in. "Baby?"

"Hi, Daddy."

"I want to show you something," Jack said cautiously. He ducked his head back out. Andie heard a rustling noise and saw him smoothing something he was holding on a hanger.

She wondered if he'd picked up some new overalls or maybe a secondhand raincoat—or maybe someone had given him a suit, which would have been great. She smiled expectantly and sat up in bed. And he walked in holding a big pink dress.

At first Andie thought he was grinning that way because he'd gotten some new shower curtain or a bedspread on sale. "What is it?" she asked, bewildered.

"It's just a little something I picked up for you," he answered, and that's when she saw that it was a dress. "It's a little busy, but you can do something with it."

He brought it over to her. She stood up and looked at it, feeling the fabric. It was awful.

"You know your mom always wore pink," he said.

Andie nodded, speechless.

"And she looked beautiful. You're going to look even better."

Andie couldn't face him. She looked back at the dress. Jack leaned over and kissed the top of her head. Then, grinning, he started for the door.

"Daddy?"

He stopped. Still smiling, he looked at her, waiting for her to speak.

"Where'd you get the money for this?" she asked.

Jack froze. Andie looked away. She knew she shouldn't have said it.

"It wasn't that much," he said—hurt, nervous. "I had some money."

Andie knew she shouldn't say it. *Don't*, she told herself. But it came out anyway: "From your new job?" She looked up at him. It was the least she could do—face him.

He stared at her blankly for a minute, then nodded sadly and sighed.

"You know, huh?"

She didn't tell him she'd known all along. "I came home before work on Wednesday. Your car was here," she said.

"Yeah. I know."

"You didn't have to lie to me."

"Yeah," he said, "I did." He leaned against her desk. "I had a line on something," he said, toying with the feather on the end of her pink pen. "But I missed the appointment."

Andie nodded. "Why'd you miss the appointment?"

"I don't know. It slipped my mind."

"It didn't slip your mind," she said softly.

"Yeah, it did."

"You didn't want the job. You only went because I forced you to. Am I right?"

"What's the point, Andie?" Jack asked tiredly.

"You gave up. She left you and you gave

up. All you want to do is wait for her to come back."

"So?" he said. "So what? I'm fifty-five, I'm not in a position to start my life over. I'm getting by okay. I work when I need to. I'm happy. You're taken care of. Things are going fine for me. It's all right."

"Why can't you forget her, Daddy?"

"It's late. You have school tomorrow." Jack set down the pen and turned to go.

"Don't walk out of this," Andie urged him softly. But he kept going, heading for the door. "Daddy!" she shouted.

He looked back at her.

"Listen to me. Please. Just listen."

"I've been all through this, Andie. You wanted me to go down to the employment place and I went and they aren't going to find nothing for someone like me. I'm too old and too tired. I don't want to go through it all again."

"Every day," she said. "You go through it every day! When are you going to stop? When are you going to wake up and realize she's really gone? She's never coming back, Daddy. Never! She's never coming back!"

"Andie, stop it!" he hollered.

But she couldn't now. "She's gone!" she shouted. "She's gone!"

Jack grabbed her.

"She *is*, Daddy. You know she is. She's not coming back." Sudden tears were streaming down her face. "Why can't you believe it?" she cried. "Why?"

Jack pulled her close to him and held her. "Because I love her," he said finally.

"She didn't love you. She didn't love me. She really didn't."

"She did," Jack said.

Andie broke away from him. "No," she said with certainty. "It's okay." She took a deep breath. "I knew it a long time ago. I felt it. When she didn't come home, I knew why. I was thirteen and I knew it. You were fifty and you didn't. Daddy, you can't live with a ghost in your heart."

Jack stepped away from her. He looked as if she'd slapped him.

"She left us," Andie said. "We didn't leave her. There was nothing we could do. It just happened. You've been in a state of shock for nearly five years. You're hurting yourself for something she did. You loved her. I loved her. She just didn't love us back, Daddy. We didn't do anything wrong. It isn't a crime to love someone."

Jack looked at her at last. "I always thought things would change," he said.

"You always *hoped* things would change."

"Yeah. There's a difference, I guess."

"I think so," Andie said.

He held open his arms to her. "A kid isn't supposed to know more than her father," he said, as she moved into them. He squeezed her tight. His throat was full of tears. Tears of sadness or pride, he couldn't say. "I'm one dumb, stubborn old man," he rasped.

"And you need a shave," she said, her voice nearly as thick with tears as his.

"And I need a shave."

He kissed her cheek and then wiped his own with the back of his hand. "You better get to bed. You've got school. I'd better hit the hay myself. I've got a few things to do tomorrow."

Andie wiped away a tear and smiled at him as he headed toward the door.

"If you don't like the dress, I'll understand. I just wanted you to know I care about you. Okay?"

She nodded. "Okay."

He opened the door, then paused. "I was going to pop for some shoes, but I didn't know your size," he said. He winked at her, and left.

Andie walked over to the dresser and pulled a handful of tissues from the box. She glanced at the picture of the girl in the pink prom gown. Then she gently took it out of the mirror and slipped it into the top drawer of the dresser. It lay there, face down, on the silk scarf she'd worn around her neck the night at The Hunt Club with Blane. A bit of straw she hadn't noticed clung to the scarf. She picked it up and rubbed it against her cheek.

Then she walked back to her bed and sat down, staring at the telephone. He hadn't called. Next to the phone was the small framed photograph of her mother—the mother she remembered, not the prom girl she'd never met.

Andie looked at the picture. She picked it up and looked at it, and thought about Blane.

And then she thought about what she'd said to her father. Her own words came back to her and, looking at the picture, it was almost as if her mother was saying them to her: "You didn't do anything wrong. It isn't a crime to love someone."

Fifteen

Steff McKee was parked out in front of the school waiting for her. The minute she saw him, Andie knew what had happened. She knew it so absolutely that her eyes misted over. She pretended she had gotten dirt in them, and wiped her eyes, and kept on going.

Steff was standing at his car. The motor was running. He opened the door as she walked by and looked at her long and hard, grinning, letting her know she was still welcome to join him. When she passed, he slammed the Porsche's door and made a gun of his hand. "Bang," he said. He didn't follow her with his eyes. He just stared straight ahead.

She didn't see Blane until mid-afternoon. She was at the other end of the hallway when she saw him coming out of a class. He was solemn, quiet. He looked preoccupied as he headed up the hall toward her. She saw him nodding without enthusiasm, acknowledging friends who called out to him as he worked his way through the crowded corridor. She knew he hadn't seen her.

138

His shoulders were hunched, his hands in his pockets, his head down. He carried his books under one arm—the way he'd carried the six-pack of beer at Steff McKee's party, Andie remembered.

She stopped walking and waited for him. Finally he saw her. His step faltered. He slowed down, and his face tightened with guilt.

The hall began to thin out as the passing period neared its end. Blane moved slowly toward her. He couldn't look at her. He kept turning his eyes to the floor. Andie watched him steadily without flinching.

All but a few kids were left hurrying to their classes. The bell rang. Blane nervously closed the distance between them.

Andie waited.

He tried to look at her, but he couldn't meet her gaze for any length of time. It was like the first time she'd seen him at Trax, she thought. He'd been nervous then, too, and having a hard time looking her in the eye.

No. Andie knew it wasn't anything like that first time. It was nothing like that at all.

Blane looked up at her and tried to smile. He didn't make it. He had to look away again. Finally there was only about a foot between them.

"How are you?" he said, shifting his feet, shifting his eyes.

"Why haven't you called me?" she asked. Her voice was clipped and cold. She scarcely recognized it. Still, she was grateful for any sound at all. For a moment she had doubted that she'd be able to speak.

"I'm really sorry. I got nailed for being in the stables," he said, looking down at his feet. "A groom must have seen us. It's against club policy, it's like a major breach. . . ." He looked up, at last, and flinched at her steady gaze.

She didn't take her eyes off him. "I called you three times. I left messages."

"My family's kind of irresponsible when it comes to things like that."

"I waited for you this morning."

"You did? Where?"

"Parking lot."

"Really?" he said, playing dumb.

"What about the Prom, Blane?" Andie said. She was tired of the game.

He leaned against a locker. She didn't move. "This is such a terrible day," he began.

"What about the Prom?" she repeated.

"I'm really late for class. Can we meet after school?" He pushed off from the locker and took a step back.

"No!" she shouted, surprising herself. "What about the Prom?"

Blane exhaled loud and hard. "This isn't the time or the place to talk." He reached out for her hand. She pulled it away.

"Say it, Blane," she said.

"Say what?"

"Say it!"

"Andie, please . . ." He looked her straight in the eye and took a deep breath. "About a month ago I asked somebody else. I forgot, and . . ."

Before she knew what she was doing, she had thrown her hand out and shoved him into the lockers. "You're a liar!"

He was stunned.

"You're a disgusting, filthy, no-good liar. You don't have the guts to tell me the truth!"

"I'm not lying," Blane protested weakly.

She crashed him into the locker again. "Tell me the truth!" she shouted.

"What?"

Andie slapped his face.

"Stop it!"

She drew back to hit him again. He grabbed her wrist.

"Tell me!" she said.

A classroom door opened, and a teacher peered out into the hall at them.

Andie ripped her wrist free and slapped Blane. "Tell me!" she shouted. "I want to hear you say it!"

"No!" he hollered back.

Two more teachers came out of their classrooms. Students began to crowd the doorways. Andie was panting, wild with rage. Her teeth were clenched. Blane was white with shock. He closed his eyes as she slapped him again.

Mr. Donnelly pushed through the crowd. "Andie!" he shouted. She didn't even hear him. She pushed back from Blane.

"You're ashamed to be seen with me! You're ashamed to go out with me! You're afraid! You're terrified that your rich friends won't approve! You're scared to death you'll lose Steff!"

Blane shook his head. "No, Andie. No. I'm sorry."

"Tell me it's true!" She grabbed his hair and held his head to the locker. "Say it!" She twisted his hair. "SAY IT!"

"It's not about you!" Blane wailed.

She released him and backed away.

"Can I explain?" he cried miserably.

Andie turned to the gathering crowd and glared at them. She heaved her books down the hall at them and walked off.

Blane yelled after her, "Andie! It's not about you!" Fighting back tears, he straightened his hair and looked at the stunned, silent crowd. Then he took a breath and walked away.

Mr. Donnelly bowed his head and rubbed his neck. He leaned down and picked up one of Andie's books. He stood holding it for a long time, looking down the hall after her.

Steff McKee had watched it all from a classroom doorway. He thought about what he'd done, and shook his head imperceptibly. It was sad but unavoidable, he decided. He figured he'd done what he had to do.

Duckie Dale had seen and heard the whole thing, too. Now he saw Blane McDonough walk past. Duckie turned and looked back at Andie. She hadn't seen him. She was walking away. She was almost out of sight now. Duckie moved away from the wall and followed Blane.

* * *

Blane was sitting on a window bench near the freaks' courtyard. The door to the yard was open, and he could see outside. He could see the empty bench on which Andie usually sat sketching and eating her lunch.

Steff McKee was standing across the hall watching Blane. "Hey, forget it, man. It's not worth getting upset over," he said.

"Just take off, okay?" Blane said, his voice breaking with emotion. "I don't need any more advice from you."

Steff ignored him. "Any girl that did that to me, I wouldn't be too jazzed to hold onto."

Blane looked across at him, then got up and headed off down the hall.

"It's not worth it, Blane," Steff called after him. "I told you it wouldn't work."

Blane didn't look up or turn around. He just kept on walking away.

"She was, is, and always will be nothing!" Steff shouted.

Blane pushed open the front doors and walked out of the school.

Disgusted, Steff shook his head. He lunged off the wall, looked down the corridor where Blane had exited, and then looked the other way.

Duckie was standing at the end of the hall. Steff started toward him. "You got a problem, bozo?" he said.

Duckie watched Steff approaching for a moment. Then he began to move toward him.

Face hard and angry, eyes set and filled with rage, Duckie charged forward. His hands closed into fists. Glaring at Steff McKee, staring straight at him, Duckie broke into a run.

Steff McKee's brow furrowed for a moment as he tried to figure out what was going on. Then his eyes widened and flashed with fear.

Duckie came at him, hightops slapping the floor, running flat out. His mouth opened wide. He screamed. It was a war-cry. And it scared the hell out of Steff McKee, who fell to the floor almost before Duckie landed on him. Steff's arms came up over his head. He cowered under his hands. Duckie was exploding. Screaming, punching, kicking, he unleashed a frenzy of rage.

Squirming beneath him, Steff whimpered in terror. "Stop! He's crazy! Help! Get him off me!" he screamed.

Classroom doors burst open. Teachers and students spilled out. Two male teachers descended on Duckie, tore him off Steff, and heaved him against the lockers. Duckie whirled around, slammed his fist into a locker door, and took off down the hall.

Steff McKee uncovered his face and looked up. They were all staring at him, teachers and students—freaks, richies, jocks, zoids, nerdy hall monitors with calculators on their belts. Their faces were aghast.

He hadn't thrown one punch. He hadn't landed a fist or laid a finger on Duckie Dale.

He'd taken a beating at the hands of a wimp. And the entire student body had witnessed it.

Down the hall, Duckie leapt into the air and snagged the Prom banner. He ripped it down, waved it with a wild shriek, then tossed it aside and kept on going.

Sixteen

It wasn't until she saw the setting sun glinting off the window of Hong's Laundry that Andie realized where she was and what she wanted. She'd been driving aimlessly for hours. She'd shuddered and shouted, wept and cursed. She'd even turned on the windshield wipers, she realized now, although it hadn't been rain that had blurred her vision; it had been her tears.

Her eyes felt swollen, and her cheeks felt starchy and raw where the tears had dried. She shut off the windshield wipers, parked the car, and sat there for a few minutes thinking things over. Finally she got out of the car, took a deep breath, and climbed the stairs to Iona's place.

A man answered Iona's door. A man in his mid-thirties, wearing a suit and tie—a nice, normal-looking suit and tie, a nice, normal-looking man—opened the door to Iona's apartment. It was a human male so clean and healthy that Andie thought she'd knocked at the wrong door.

He must have read her mind or seen her jaw drop. He said, "Andie?"

She was startled that he knew her name.

"You're Andie?" he said again, extending his hand to her.

Dazed, she shook his hand. "Yeah. How do you know me?"

"The hair, the eyes," he said. "And the earrings. They're pink. Iona told me. Come on in."

Baffled, Andie stepped into the apartment.

"I'm Terrance," he said. "She's in the bedroom getting ready. Why don't you go tell her to shake a tailfeather? We're late."

She nodded mutely and backed away toward the bedroom. The door was partway open. Andie peeked in. "Iona?" she called.

"Andie? Come on in."

She stepped inside, and Iona came out of the bathroom. Andie couldn't believe her eyes.

Gone were the beehive, the leather and chains, the blood-red lips and darkly painted eyes. Iona looked as soft and new, as vulnerable and pretty as she had the other day dancing in her prom gown. And she was wearing a dress. A nice, normal-looking dress. Iona saw Andie's stunned expression and actually blushed.

"Laugh," she said, "and I'll deck you."

"What happened?"

Iona gave her a kiss. "Either I fell in love or it's all those drugs I took in the Sixties coming back on me." She stepped back and did a half-turn. "What do you think? Honestly?"

"Honestly? You look great," Andie said.

"I look like a mother."

"Kind of. But that's okay. You look happy."

"I am. It's weird, but I really think I am. You met Terrance?"

Andie nodded.

"He's a Yuppie," Iona said, "but he's so nice. And he's gentle, and employed. I'm so far ahead of the game, I can't tell you. Next time you see me, I may be picking out baby names."

Andie laughed softly. Iona tipped her chin up. "You all right?"

Andie nodded mutely. She was afraid that if she tried to talk she might burst out crying.

"No, you're not," Iona said. "What is it?"

Andie shook her head.

"Oh, God, baby," Iona said, "am I blowing your mind? Just the outside's changed, Andie. Inside, I'm still crazy."

Andie tried to smile. It didn't work. Her lips began to quiver. Iona took one look. "Uh-oh. Boy trouble?" she said.

Andie's eyes filled with tears again.

"The worst?" Iona asked gently.

"Way beyond. He backed out on me," she whispered. "He said he asked somebody and forgot about it."

"I'm so sorry."

"It's okay," Andie said, and moved gratefully into Iona's arms.

"You know how you told me that if I wanted your prom dress, I could have it?" she whispered.

"Yeah, but—"

"I need it, Iona," she said, wiping her tears. "I want it."

"Sure. It's yours. But why?"

"I just need it."

Iona nodded and got the dress from her closet without a word.

"I love you," Andie said.

"It's mutual," said Iona, laying the dress across her arms. "Only, listen. Get it cleaned. It smells of twenty-year-old Budweiser."

On Tuesday night Andie took Iona's pink formal off the hook on the back of her bedroom door, where she'd hung it the night before. She took it off the hanger and out of the cleaning bag, unwrapped it, and laid it down on her bed. For a while, she circled the bed studying the dress. She smoothed the skirt, ran her fingers over the lace bodice and long sleeves. Then she picked up the dress and held it in front of her and studied herself in the dresser mirror. And then she put Iona's pink formal away.

On Wednesday night, Andie took the dress her father had bought for her out of her closet, shook it, and slipped it on over the t-shirt and shorts she was wearing. She put her hands on the gown's waistline and bunched it in front of the mirror. Then she took off the pink gown and laid it out on her bed, and got Iona's formal and put it down alongside the new gown.

She looked at each dress separately. She looked at them together. She pulled the artificial rose off the dress her father had bought and held it in her teeth while she got her sketchpad and some charcoal pencils. Then she leaned against the wall near her bed and began to sketch.

Long after midnight she stopped drawing. She took the flower out of her mouth, hung up the dresses, and went to sleep.

On Thursday night, after she'd made the rounds of her favorite thriftshops and variety stores and picked up some choice pieces of costume jewelry, glittery pins, and antique ribbons, Andie began to rip, cut, match, and sew the dresses. She studied the sketches she'd made. She checked the magazine photos she'd pinned to her wall. And once she even drew out her mother's prom picture and held it up next to one of the sketches she'd done before putting it back in her dresser.

On Friday night Andie dreamed about her mother. But this time her mother was wearing a dress and not the pink gown she usually wore in Andie's dreams. She was wearing a nice, normal-looking dress, just like Iona's. And this time she wasn't in the big stone mansion with the white pillars and circular driveway anymore. She was standing on the porch of a squat, one-story bungalow, which had been painted white. It looked small, but sweet and clean and bright. There were rosebushes in the little front yard, and the fence around the house had been fixed. It had became a white picket fence surrounding a tiny, beautiful green lawn that ended at the base of the pink rosebushes.

In the dream, Andie said, "Don't worry about me. I'll be fine."

Her mother nodded and said, "Of course you will. You didn't do anything wrong, baby." And then her mother turned into Iona. And Iona was dancing in her pink prom gown, dancing on the white porch of the little bungalow. She looked beautiful and happy and young.

Andie turned to her father in the dream. He was standing on the porch now. And she said, "Look at her, Daddy."

He looked at the girl in the prom gown. He smiled. He put his arm around Andie's shoulder and said, "She looks pretty in pink." And the girl whirled around. And she was Andie.

On Saturday night Jack set his camera down on the table in the living room. The flash went off unexpectedly. Cursing under his breath, he picked it up and examined it to see what was wrong.

"Daddy," Andie called.

Jack looked up and smiled. He bent to pick up the camera. Then his eyes snapped back up to Andie. "Oh, my Lord," he breathed.

She was standing in the doorway wearing the loveliest pink dress he'd ever seen. It didn't look anything like the one he'd bought her. On the other hand, it didn't look anything like the one she'd gotten from Iona, either. It was as simple, unique, and beautiful as the willowy young woman wearing it. And it took him a moment to realize that an hour ago the exquisite young woman had been his little girl.

151

He walked to her and kissed her. She held him tight.

"Look at you," Jack said. "When your guy walks in that door, he's going to drop dead."

Andie's smile faded. She shook her head. "No, he won't."

"Like hell—" he began.

"He won't because he's not coming."

"What?" Jack said.

"He's not coming, Daddy. He backed out on me. His friends pressured him into it. He's not very strong."

"Who do they think they are?" Jack demanded furiously.

"It doesn't matter who they think they are," Andie said, putting a silencing finger on his lips. "It's just high school, Daddy. It's okay."

Jack looked down at his shoes. He tapped his foot, trying to control his anger.

"I'm going to go," Andie said softly.

He stared at her, looking completely perplexed.

"Daddy, I want to do it. I'm not sad about it. I'm not hurt," she said. Then she smiled. "Well, I mean, I am hurt, a little, but this is something I have to do. If I don't do it, I'll feel a lot worse. Okay? I'm fine. I'm just fine. I'll go. I'll walk in and I'll come home."

Jack was silent.

"To let them know they didn't break me," she said.

He would have run away, he knew, from what she was determined to face. He might be frightened, but she wasn't. He stared at her, his heart bursting with pride, his eyes flooding. He nodded with understanding, and she kissed his cheek.

"I want them to know I'm proud of who I am. I'm proud of where I come from. I'm proud of you."

He took her in his arms and held her close. "I love you, honey," he said.

"I know," she whispered. "I love you too." And then she kissed his cheek again, and picked up her car keys, and walked out the door.

"Andie!" he called after her.

She was heading toward her car. She turned around. He was standing on the porch, just the way he had been in her dream.

He grinned at her and raised his fist. "Give 'em hell, baby," he shouted.

Seventeen

The hotel was old and elegant. Crystal chandeliers and wall sconces lit the ballroom. The rich mahogany dance floor gleamed. The orchestra on the bandstand wore white dinner jackets. As they launched into the first slow number of the evening, starry-eyed Prom couples drifted onto the floor.

Near the bandstand Blane McDonough, distant and distracted, looked across the ballroom. Kate Hanson stood behind him, talking to friends. She turned to him and smiled. Lost in thought, Blane didn't see her.

On the other side of the vast room Steff McKee caught sight of Blane through the milling crowd. Once they had been best friends. Now the friendship was dead, cold, an historical fact.

"Oh, God, excruciating!" Benny squealed. She tugged Steff's elbow. "Look at that. Chessy Edwards and Melly Gaites have the same dress. Trauma time."

Steff ignored her. Blane had just seen him. From across the ballroom, Blane had glanced at Steff. His face was utterly passive, empty. No guilt, no remorse, no anxiety. No anger. Steff tried to hold Blane's look. But there was nothing to hold onto. Finally he shook it off and turned to Benny, her friends, and their dates.

"As soon as anybody's ready to go upstairs and get serious, let me know," he said, without enthusiasm.

"We just got here!" Benny complained.

"We can go up and come back down, you know."

Benny rubbed against his arm. "Did you look at the suite?"

"It's okay," Steff said.

"*Okay?*" She shoved him playfully. "Just okay?"

"It's five hundred bucks a night. It's not going to be a palace, Ben. Come on."

Benny smoothed the skirt of her gown and hiked up her elbow-length gloves. "I think we should stay down here for awhile," she said, her voice both arrogant and whiny. "We're not going to see a lot of these people much longer. It's kind of the end, okay?" He paid no attention to her, so she kissed his cheek coquettishly. "Okay?"

It was "kind of the end," Steff knew. And some end it had turned out to be. His friendship with Blane McDonough was over. He'd lost his best friend, lost what should have been a great evening, lost what was supposed to be a memorable event in his life. And what was his consolation prize? Benny Trombley.

His temper flared for a moment. "I don't

155

care what you do," he growled at her. He reached into his tuxedo pocket and withdrew an old silver flask. The family flask, he thought bitterly. His dad had passed it to him tonight with the keys to the Rolls. "But don't get too polluted," his father had advised. "You'll want to remember this one for a long time."

Right, Steff thought, shaking his head in disgust, as he unscrewed the top of the flask. It was shaping up to be a really memorable night. Right. Really.

All alone, Andie walked down the long hallway leading to the ballroom. The hotel carpeting was thick and soft under her feet. She moved slowly, holding her head up, clutching her gloves and evening bag. At the end of the carpeted corridor, the massive double doors were closed. She heard the music spilling from the room.

It was now or never, she knew. She slowed down, and stopped. She had to decide whether or not she really wanted to go through with this. She'd been so calm up until now, right up until she'd seen the closed doors and heard the music and the voices and laughter coming from the ballroom.

If she waited at the door, listening from now until forever, she would not hear the voice of a single friend inside that room—not one person who would welcome her, be happy to see her, or even be willing to talk to her. Not one person would think of her as anything but an intruder.

What was she doing here? What was she trying to prove? It was her Senior Prom. But Seniors like Andie Walsh were not expected to attend.

Jack sat out on the porch, breathing in the night air. It occurred to him that it would be nice to have some rosebushes around the place. Catherine had loved pink roses, and a long, long time ago, he'd planted a rosebush out front for her. It was just a scraggly thing, and it had frozen up during the winter. But he remembered that it had produced two perfect pink roses before it died. He thought maybe, when he got a real job, he'd buy a nice healthy new little rosebush for the place. Only this time he'd wrap it up good, in burlap, against the frost.

Andie would probably be gone by then—off to college in the East, he guessed. Which reminded him that he was free to move on if he wanted to. He could head west and look for work.

Jack pulled a cigarette out of the pack in his shirt pocket and lit up in the darkness. In the matchlight, he saw the peeling porch railing. He thought: "Nothing a few coats of white paint couldn't help." And then he thought maybe he could get started on that part right away. Take a couple of days to scrape the splinters and rot off the railing. Maybe he'd start tomorrow morning.

God knew he had enough gallons of outdoor white sitting in the shed behind the house.

He'd planned to paint the place the summer before Catherine left. He'd planned to do a whole lot of things before she'd taken off. Maybe if he'd done some of them, she'd still be around.

Maybe not.

Well, what was he thinking of? Hadn't he just told himself he was free? Few months down the road he could take off same as she had. See a bit of life, bum, work, do what he pleased.

Sitting on the top step, he leaned back against the porch railing and blew a smoke ring up into the night. Then he smiled, thinking about Mrs. Burson down at the employment office, thinking about how he'd blown a ring past her ear that first time. She'd turned out to be okay. He was sure she'd come up with something for him soon. And this time, smoke rings were all he'd blow. He wouldn't blow the job, that was for sure.

A couple of rosebushes to sweeten the night air. Throw a rug of grass sod over the dusty old yard. Paint the porch, straighten up the picket fence.

There. He'd gone and done it again. Why was he thinking of cleaning up the old place? It was time to move on, wasn't it?

And then he thought, well, maybe just until he moved on. Maybe he could paint it and pretty it up, and he and Andie could have their last summer together in the house. Maybe he could give her a house she didn't need to be ashamed of. And a father she could be proud of, too.

He took a deep drag on the cigarette, started to cough, and tossed it away suddenly, down into the dirt. Then he stood up and ground the butt out under his heel. And then, for no reason at all, he smiled. He rubbed his big calloused hands together and stomped back around to the back of the house to the shed. He pulled the flashlight down off its hook and shone it on the cans of paint, the tools and yard rakes all stashed back there.

He thought of his little girl, all grown up now. He thought of how beautiful she'd looked tonight. He thought of how amazingly brave she was, and smart and bound to make something of herself in the world. And he thought, well, might as well get started now—right now, tonight.

Fighting tears, Andie took a step backward. She knew she was on the verge of bolting from the hotel. For a second her hands curled into defiant fists. Then all at once she let out her breath. Her shoulders drooped. She'd lost her nerve.

"Oh, no," she whispered. "No," and angrily she brushed away a tear. "Damn it, damn it, damn it," she murmured, whirling away from the door and turning to leave. She took a step, then stopped and looked down the hall.

At the far end of the mezzanine was a boy.

He was tall, lean, striking. A boy in a sleek black tuxedo, dark hair swept back, sunglasses.

Andie stared at him. She peered hard down the corridor.

The boy peeled off his sunglasses and revealed himself.

Andie's mouth fell open. "Duckie?" she breathed.

She was stunned. After all that had happened, all the pain she'd caused him, he had come to be with her. He really did love her. Under the strange clothes, the weird behavior, the quirks and eccentricities was the strongest, truest, and most noble friend she'd ever have.

"Oh, God," she murmured. And then she started to cry.

Smiling, Duckie moved down the hall toward her.

She met him midway along the corridor and threw her arms around him.

"What happened?" she asked.

"You're looking at it," Duckie whispered against her hair.

"I can't believe this."

"You know what else you won't believe—I aced my history paper. I'm going to graduate, Andie."

He held her at arm's length. "You look breathtaking," he said. She laughed and hugged him again.

"I want you to know," he said, as she stepped back, "that despite the new coiffure and the duds, I remain the Duck Man."

He pointed to his feet. Andie looked down. Duckie was still wearing his ancient hightops.

"May *I* admire *you?*" Andie said softly through her tears.

"If you wish," he said, and she laughed.

Duckie Dale looked at her with his ice-melting grin, his dark eyes dancing with pleasure at the sight of her. He offered his arm, and they started down the hall together to the ballroom.

The doors opened as they approached, and Mr. Donnelly came out. It took him a moment to recognize them, but when he did, his whole face lit with surprise and admiration. He shook his head in wonder and stood back, holding open the door for them.

"This thing is so uncomfortable," Duckie said to him, tugging at his collar. "I could never be a waiter."

Mr. Donnelly smiled. "Glad you could make it," he said.

Nearly frozen with nerves, Andie nodded.

Duckie patted her hand on his arm. "You okay?" he asked as they stepped over the threshold into the music and noise of the elegant old ballroom.

"No," she said.

"Good. Just checking."

They walked in. The crowd surrounding the dance floor, the couples standing and talking and laughing, turned toward them one at a time, and then in twos, threes, and fours—growing silent, stunned, clearing a path as they passed. They stepped up to the edge of the dance floor, and the people who saw them stopped dancing.

Blane was among them. He looked over his shoulder to see what the others were staring at—and then he dropped Kate Hanson's hand. He stopped dancing and turned toward Duckie and Andie. He was mesmerized.

Kate looked at Andie. Then she looked back at Blane. And then she crossed her arms peevishly. Blane was smiling at Andie Walsh.

Andie was smiling, too, though she hadn't seen him. She looked across the dance floor, not focusing on anybody, just feeling Duckie's hand on hers—just knowing he was with her, and smiling.

Benny had her eyes closed and her head on Steff's shoulder. When he stopped dancing, she opened her eyes lazily. Then she gasped. Steff stepped away from her. All activity on the dance floor stopped. People were just standing still, looking at Andie and Duckie.

The music from the bandstand petered out. The orchestra had stopped playing, and the musicians were craning around to see what had halted the dancers.

Andie and Duckie stood proud in the silent ballroom, all eyes on them.

And then, finally, someone moved. The crowd parted. And Blane McDonough walked slowly toward them.

Behind him, Kate was hissing, "No, don't. Come back." And some of his crowd were whispering. "Whew, he's out of it, man," one guy said. "What's he doing? Isn't she the one who went berserk on him in the hall?"

But Blane kept going. Andie saw him, and he kept on looking and walking toward her, and she didn't turn away. And Duckie, watching Blane approach, knew he had nothing to fear, nothing to risk. In a way, he admired Blane for coming over.

Blane offered his hand to Duckie. Duckie looked at it, then at Blane. Finally he shook Blane's hand. And then Duckie squeezed Andie's hand, released her, and walked away. He stepped over to the bandstand to the conductor, determined to get the music started again.

Blane smiled at Andie. For the first time since he'd seen her in the halls at school, he knew that he was good enough for her. For the first time he was able to meet her strength and honesty with his own. He saw her smile. He saw her eyes accept his gesture, his unspoken apology, his admiration and love. And then he turned away.

Duckie was back by then. Andie took his hand and walked him out to the dance floor. The crowd separated around them again, leaving Andie and Duckie alone at the center of the floor.

She took Duckie in her arms. The orchestra began to play again. Duckie grinned. And then his face froze with terror.

"Andie," he whispered, "I can't *dance*."

"Neither can I," she said through her unwavering smile.

"Are we crazy?"

"Completely."

She took a deep breath and began to move to the music. Duckie followed clumsily. A few steps—and they began to loosen up. A few steps and they were dancing without shame or concern for what anybody thought.

Blane thought Andie had made this night a real graduation night for him. He watched her, his eyes brimming with pleasure at her graceful beauty. He knew he'd probably never see her again, but his heart was warmed by how right he had been to choose her and how much she had taught him about courage and self-respect.

Benny thought Andie had stolen the Prom. Flabbergasted and furious, she glared across the dance floor at the misfit who'd become the main attraction, the transformed freak in the amazing pink prom gown, the rag-hag who'd turned into the Makeover-of-the-Month. "I could've had that gown," she told one of her friends. "She got it at Magique. She practically ripped it out of my hands and ran out of the store with it. You should have seen her. She knocked everything over. Ask Kate."

Steff thought this might be the worst night of his life. First, he'd lost Andie to Blane, his best friend. Of course now he'd lost Blane, too. And then there was Duckie Dale, the biggest loser the school had ever seen—except for the one time the jerk had thrown a lucky punch at

Steff McKee and the whole school had turned out to witness it. Now Steff had to stand here and watch his ex-best friend and the frog, or Duck—who'd all of a sudden turned into Prince of the Prom—drooling all over Andie Walsh. Or did he? No way, man. Steff grabbed Benny's arm. "I'm bored," he said. "Let's split." And he led her out of the ballroom.

Kate saw Benny and Steff leaving. "They've ruined everything," she pouted. "The entire Prom. Steff and Benny just left. What are you grinning at, Blane? Honest to God, I don't understand you."

Blane wasn't grinning. He was smiling. And so were Andie Walsh and Duckie Dale. They held each other as the couples around them began to dance again. They held each other and smiled. They danced around and around, smiling at each other, then laughing, dancing around and around and around, until they were one—one whirling, smiling, laughing blur of pink.

THE LATEST BOOKS IN THE BANTAM BESTSELLING TRADITION

☐	25561	**GODDESS** Margaret Pemberton	$3.95
☐	25315	**FRIEND** Diana Henstell	$3.95
☐	23638	**THE OTHER SIDE** Diana Henstell	$3.50
☐	25379	**THE PROUD BREED** Celeste DeBlasis	$4.50
☐	24937	**WILD SWAN** Celeste DeBlasis	$3.95
☐	05092	**SWAN'S CHANCE** Celeste DeBlasis (A Bantam Hardcover)	$16.95
☐	25314	**THE LONG WAY HOME** Alan Ebert w/Janice Rotchstein	$3.95
☐	22838	**TRADITIONS** Alan Ebert w/Janice Rotchstein	$3.95
☐	24866	**PROMISES AND LIES** Susanne Jaffe	$4.50
☐	24112	**MADNESS OF A SEDUCED WOMAN** Susan Fromberg Schaeffer	$3.95
☐	23981	**THE LITTLE DRUMMER GIRL** J. LeCarré	$3.95
☐	23920	**VOICE OF THE HEART** Barbra Taylor Bradford	$4.50
☐	24515	**DANCER OF DREAMS** Patricia Matthews	$3.50
☐	23846	**FAMILY TIES** Syrell Rogovin Leahy	$3.95
☐	25917	**MISTRAL'S DAUGHTER** Judith Krantz	$4.95
☐	25609	**PRINCESS DAISY** Judith Krantz	$4.95

Prices and availability subject to change without notice.

DON'T MISS
THESE CURRENT
Bantam Bestsellers

Experience all the passion and adventure life has to offer in these bestselling novels by and about women.

BANTAM
SHOP-AT-HOME
C·A·T·A·L·O·G

Special Offer
Buy a Bantam Book
for only 50¢.

Now you can have an up-to-date listing of Bantam's hundreds of titles plus take advantage of our unique and exciting bonus book offer. A special offer which gives you the opportunity to purchase a Bantam book for only 50¢. Here's how!

By ordering any five books at the regular price per order, you can also choose any other single book listed (up to a $4.95 value) for just 50¢. Some restrictions do apply, but for further details why not send for Bantam's listing of titles today!

Just send us your name and address and we will send you a catalog!